Classroom Circus

A Week in the Exam Factory

Coco Wilde

To my dearest A, who has faced many challenges growing up as the child of a teacher. I dedicate this book to you with all my heart. As a teacher, I know that my dedication to my profession meant that I didn't always have the time to give you the attention you deserved. But please know that despite this, you have always been an amazing person, and I am so proud of the person you have become. Your strength, resilience, and unwavering spirit have been an inspiration to me and have kept me going during the tough times. As a teacher's child, you know firsthand about the unique challenges faced by children of educators, and I want to thank you for your understanding and support. You are fabulous, and I hope that this book will inspire and uplift you.

With all my love, Mama xoxo.

PROLOGUE

Once upon a time, teachers were respected and admired for their knowledge and ability to shape young minds. But today, some blame teachers for everything. It's like they're the punching bag for society's shortcomings. Despite overcrowded classrooms, limited resources, and a lack of appreciation, teachers still show up every day to make a difference in their students' lives. So, let's peek into a teacher's life for a week and see if it is an easy job.

MONDAY, 3:45 PM

"Move back! Move back! Move behind the tape!" roared the bleary-eyed policeman with frustration. His face had not met a razor in days, and the bags under his eyes told the story of another public sector worker who was overtired, undervalued and hardly paid enough for the donkeywork he had to endure. Opposite him, Hoodie Boy, so christened by me because of the black hood he wore daily over his short blonde curls, followed his urge to be aggressive.

"You can't tell me what to do!"

The policemen's eyes narrowed.

"Yes, I can. And if you don't listen, I will arrest you."

What a compelling statement. *Yes, I can. And if you don't listen, I will arrest you. Arrest you. Wow. Yes, please do it!* I wanted to witness this arrest. I wanted to help with this arrest —a citizen's arrest done by me. I had always dreamt of a job in law enforcement. There was my chance. I kept screaming in my head, hoping a speech bubble would magically form over me and the man in uniform would notice it and act upon it. Hoodie Boy and his hangers-on, who existed in intellectual quarantine, had just run off the factory grounds towards the red bus that had caught fire. Their sprint coincided with the day's last bell, which released the kids back into society.

It puzzled me why so many of the kids, not just Hoodie Boy and his crew, but others, had chosen to run towards what could be identified from 100 metres away as a fire. A proper fire with flames and smoke and heat. And they did so, not to help but to look. And of course to film. Everything needed to be recorded and uploaded for the world to see. Gone were the days of secret adventures.

Please, arrest him. Please, please, please. I continued my attempts to telepathically communicate with this policeman, but his receptors were not operating. They were overstimulated by noisy school kids, residents who had stepped out of their council houses and the confused people who had escaped the inferno bus. The policeman was forced to deal with a bundle of humans, neither standing nor moving. They were simply in the way.

I longed for Hoodie Boy to be taken away. Single-handedly, he managed to stop everyone else from learning. Instead, he turned around arrogantly, acting as if this situation he was in and that he had created for himself had nothing to do with him. I had seen it more than once. He removed his six-foot lanky body from the crowds. He was bumping his inflated self-image into several people along the way. On purpose, of course. Not unusual. The common good was not his cup of tea.

So, yes, an arrest would have improved community relations immediately. But, nothing. The cycle of disruption would continue tomorrow. All I wanted was to teach like my mum used to teach when I was little, and she had allowed me to sit in the back of her class on Saturday mornings.

The dry air tickled my throat. For some time, I stood there, paralysed by exhaustion and frustration, thinking amid the crowds, hearing the fire engines in the distance. Did other teachers have similar sentiments? Did they wish for their pupils to be arrested? Probably yes. At least, this is what I told myself. Especially us serfs. We did the groundwork in the exam factories. Us *whose face,* according to Theodore Roosevelt, was *marred by dust and sweat and blood; who strives valiantly; who errs, who comes short again and again because there is no effort without error and shortcoming.* I wanted to believe that many of us classroom combatants had similar thoughts. How else would we have coped? This sarcasm was necessary. But was it even sarcasm? Sarcasm, from the Greek sarkázein, means *to strip off the flesh* or *to tear it to pieces*. I did not want to tear anyone to pieces. I was too tired for that. And neither did I want to clean up the mess. Maybe it was cynicism, *a mindset that rejects existing norms and considers them ridiculous*. Or possibly a combination of both. Cynical sarcasm? I was sure it was a survival instinct.

Somewhere, I had even read that psychologists classified this behaviour as standard, a coping mechanism for employees like us, workers placed in high-stress environments surrounded by two types of people. Firstly, the ones for whom we were primarily responsible. The kids came to the factory to be educated. Secondly, the ones who tried to micromanage our every move, driving us to insanity. Those overlords in senior positions were a different species. Roosevelt would have referred to them as *cold and timid souls who neither know victory nor defeat*. They had suckled on the milk of authority and occupied positions I did not like nor want and even less understood. The overlords' galaxy was filled with career progression, serious pay and ridiculous job titles.

The crude jokes in the car park, the suspicious glimpses in meetings, the courteous disinterest in new initiatives and the complete immersion in a fake teacher persona worn like a cloak from the first bell of the day to the last. They were features of us, the serfs in factories. Therapy was too expensive, alcohol too addictive, and gyms smelled funny. Money and time were in short supply, so my colleagues and I had to master the art of cynical sarcasm. This was our survival hack. An after-effect of thousands of hours of teaching under the jurisdiction of inspectors who had disconnected from reality and left the arena long ago. The non-teachers in my tribe regularly went into cardiac arrest, hearing us serfs reveal the ins and outs of factory life.

"Wakey, wakey!"

I felt someone's hands clap close to my eyes.

"Are you sleepwalking?"

"Yes, I am."

I had moved closer to the factory without even noticing. I looked dazed. Why else would Cara employ clapping to bring me back to the education planet?

"Let's hurry, we are late for the Year Team meeting," she said.

Good, old Cara was part of the furniture at 'Comply Or Fail Academy'. In her twenties, she had worked as an emergency nurse in New York City, faced with stabbings, gunshot wounds and other regular emergencies. Cara had seen it all. This Irish energy bundle was a learning mentor who had mastered the teacher's stare better than anyone I knew. Nothing scared or shocked Cara. Not Hoodie Boy. Not the police. Not the overlords in their high visibility vests and walkie-talkies with sticks up their back sides.

"Cara, help me understand! What had triggered the volcano of teaching to erupt into a lava of never-ending pet projects by self-proclaimed education tsars?"

"I have no idea when it all bombed, Eva. This is your territory. You are the history teacher." Cara replied.

"Is it just this island located in the low-cost streets of the education monopoly board game? You are Irish, tell me. What is it like back home?"

"To be honest, I am planning my retirement. All I remember is that the nuns at my school were prime examples of authoritarian personalities." Cara replied, her short legs picking up pace.

"Hm, it is such a petri dish of problems."

"That's a good way of phrasing it! What is it you are worried about?"

"Everything, Cara. Everything. I have nine lessons left with my GCSE kids. These kids get tested on conflicts in Asia in the 50s and 60s. Asia, a place most of them have never seen and probably will never see."

"And this is why they need you. You are their positivity injection. They need your encouragement and your *Let's do this* attitude."

"I don't know if I can do this. All I want to do is sleep."

"Don't we all?"

"Did you see Hoodie Boy? He nearly got arrested by the policeman over there. I was hoping he would be escorted away." I giggled.

"Hoodie Boy?" Cara was puzzled.

"Yes, Mikhail. I call him Hoodie Boy because of the black hoodie he keeps wearing. Clearly against the factory's uniform policy, but the overlords seem to wear a pirate mask over both eyes in his case."

Cara laughed.

"Yes, I saw him. Sooner or later, he will get arrested. Maybe he needs more hugs, you know, like Cameron suggested."

"Who is meant to do the hugging? You or I? Looks like the parents have not done it."

"Imagine, we did the hugging. We would be catapulted right into the centre of a misconduct hearing." Cara said with her eyes wide open.

“I reckon this boy will be confined in a state-funded facility and end up doing his Functional English and Maths there."

We tried to make our way through the crowds. Some younger kids admiringly hung around the older ones, waiting to see whether there was any more action. But the day's highlight was over, and it was finally time to go home. Ordinary people living next to the factory had come out to see the spectacle from the safety of their front doors. A bus on fire was not an everyday occurrence. Nobody wanted to be seen as a rubberneck. They had to act as if nothing had happened by casually taking out the rubbish and placing it in the bin located in their reasonably sized front gardens outside their 1950s council houses.

"One of my ex-colleagues worked in a prison and liked it. Apparently, the jailbirds really wanted to learn."

"You should apply. I bet the working hours are better."

"Everything must be better than 60 hours per week. There are plenty of prisons but not enough education."

I thought my mask of sanity would slip if I started to apply elsewhere and sniffed the air of being treated like a professional.

"It's not too late yet. You have until the 31st to be released by the end of August."

"I will stick it out here for a bit and then one day take Bella abroad. She can go to an international school."

"Do it. Bella will like it. Everything is better than this."

Cara nodded in the direction of the people who stood outside their houses.

"Why are all these people at home? They don't look like pensioners. What's their trick?"

I pulled up my shoulders. I had no answer. There were three overlords at the end of the road, near the factory gates, waving their arms as a signal for kids to move away.

"Ooooh, here they are. The trendsetters in their high-vis vests. Cara, did you know we worked at a building site?"

"An intellectual building site, yes! Most educational establishments have become part of the high-vis culture."

“I don’t know where mine is. Probably under a dried-out glue stick and a scrunched-up portrait drawn by a little year seven kid who is naive enough to believe I frame their masterpiece."

I felt slightly guilty for making fun of a kid. Cynical sarcasm.

"The nuns in my school never sported a high-vis. Not on trips and not in the playground, nowhere."

"In my backyard, there were no high-vis vests either. Schooling and childhood worked differently there."

“To be fair, I have seen them on road trips through Europe. Some countries have made carrying them in the car mandatory in emergencies. In exam factories, however, this is pretty new."

"You know when I feel foolish? When we have to wear them inside the building on duty. Whilst walking up and down the same corridor for 20 minutes."

"You have to do this," Cara suggested, " so kids know they can approach you as if this vest makes you more approachable. Some may hope that the vest gives them credibility, authority or power. You know how psychologists study and examine this. What do they call it again?"

"Situational variables," I remembered, "can affect obedience because authority figures often wear clothes that symbolise their position of authority. It is possible that the thinking behind those exam factory vests was not for kids to spot the grown-ups easily but for the overlords to wear something that gave them a higher status and a greater sense of legitimacy. They were hoping for the kids to obey the high-vis wearer."

"Makes sense. Most of the overlords are on a power trip anyway. They love authority and for the kids and the rest of us to be obedient."

"The few times when I didn't wear my vest, the earth kept moving, hell did not freeze over, and nothing happened. Odd, isn't it?"

"This is true. But Missy, remember, there is a clear hierarchy in the exam factories. The feudal system is still around. People need to know their place and remain there. The higher-ups in the feudal factory get to wear the cooler vests."

"Correct. Serfs like us have to make do with the flimsy little ones and the top dogs over there, the overlords. They are given proper jackets with pockets and all."

"Don't forget the walkie-talkies," Cara

interjected, "they must feel as if employed for some undercover mission, speaking to other overlord agents, trying to maintain discipline in the feudal factory society."

"Yeah, but let's face it, this is not some fancy FBI movie."

The thought of our overlords working for the FBI on special missions was comical.

"You are right. But if I am honest, Cara, I would have killed for one of those walkie-talkies back in my day, yet now in the 21st century. It's kind of embarrassing. Don't you think?"

"Not as embarrassing as the big bell I saw Maxine carry during morning break. A clear demotion. Did you see it? It was massive. Like made for cows. Maxine had to walk around like a cow in the fields."

"Yeah, and I bet as soon as the kids heard it, they walked into the factory like Pavlov's dogs."

We had arrived at the factory, and Cara walked away from me.

"Please keep a seat for me next to you. See you in a bit."

MONDAY, 4 PM

The year team meeting could wait. After a morning briefing, five lessons and an unscheduled bus fire incident that had forced most of us serfs outside to stop a riot, I needed the toilet. Whiskey would have been great, too, but it was not provided. Water would have to do. As I was humming *Tell me why I don't like Mondays* to myself, I enjoyed the emptiness of the corridors. It was almost serene. Amongst the displays about the geography trip from five years ago, one could find peace, unlike the people who were killed in the Cleveland shooting in the late 70s. The event that had inspired the song I was humming. There, Brenda did not like Mondays. Who did? Nobody. And yet, most people went about their day without shooting anyone. My last factory had a lockdown and negotiating protocol in case a terrorist left a bomb in the factory. Sure, we serfs did have a substantial set of negotiation skills. Still, those were more aligned with issues such as returning a bag or handing over a phone. Nobody, not even the overlords with the FBI-style gadgets, was really trained to negotiate with a bomber, terrorist or suicidal maniac who wanted to take a few others with them into the grave or paradise or wherever they had been told they would end up.

I deliberated how not to touch the staff toilet door to get in when it magically opened. Kirsten, the Head of English, barged out. She had not expected anyone. Why would she? We were all meant to be in meetings.

"Where have you been hiding? I have not seen you in ages."

"There is too much to do. I am on autopilot, flying from lesson to lesson, from meeting to meeting, from week to week, always hoping not to crash." Kirsten said, looking drained.

She was the perfect example of a zombie. She was a next-level zombie, as the kids would say. Kirsten could place herself on a chair in class to be a prop for a creative writing exercise in her lesson. But, standing on the chair would require a 14-page risk assessment. Because nobody had the time for that, the kids would not see Kirsten, the zombie, standing on a chair in English Year 9 on a rainy Thursday afternoon.

"I feel you. It's the same with me. I cannot wait for the summer holidays."

"And half-term. But I am probably going to be ill. I tend to get sick most half-terms. OK, I must rush. Year Team meeting. Speak later."

"Yes, I am running la ...."

The door shut on me. In the mirror, a tired reflection stared back, along with several yellow cats which formed part of the design of my dress. They really needed to start putting puppies on dresses. Cats were nasty. I experienced their viciousness when I was three, and a cat scratched me. I had swung it around by its tail, but those animals were robust. There was no need to get cranky. The fire incident had shaken me a bit.

Miss Slump already paraded up and down the English classroom until she came to a halt next to the word of the week, which stated RESILIENCE and underneath in black letters *the capacity to recover quickly from difficulties: toughness*. That was needed in life toughness, especially in an underfunded state factory; kids and staff needed it equally.

"Please look at the datasheet that is coming around and discuss with those next to you whether there are any students in the year group who you think would benefit from the anti-aggression boxing sessions with Mo."

I wondered who this Mo was. Not a serf. Probably someone from an outside agency or, better, someone who got a lot of money from the government to run an over-expensive afterschool activity that did not yield results.

As Head of Year, Miss Slump was a biggie. She

was big in size and authority but also heart. She was a good one. She loved the kids, and they did not try to kill her; some probably even liked her. Others figured that as a Head of Year, she was a higher-up in the feudal factory system. Someone to not mess around with.

I smirked at Cara, who had kept a seat right next to her in the back. We were like naughty kids. PE Andrew, energy drink in hand, who forever cracked teenage boy jokes, nodded when I sat between him and Cara.

"How many of those drinks do you consume in a day?" I whispered.

"Half a dozen. Eating is cheating, you know."

I shook my head. He was right, though. I had never seen PE staff eat. Even though they kept talking about healthy eating and were pretty fit, in the body type of way, not the looks department, I considered their diet insufficient. Anyone not on at least three main meals and three additional snacks could not be trusted. Impossible.

We all had yet to look at the datasheet we had been given.

"Ladies, it's May. We need to get the summer bodies ready."

Cara and I rolled our eyes at each other. PE Andrew preached to the wrong crowd.

"People have gone full swing into a diet frenzy just because we had five minutes of sunshine. That will not tempt me to starve myself." Cara said emotionless.

"Me neither. I refuse to keep up with the latest dieting trends."

"Exactly, Eva. Some people jump on the starvation bandwagon faster than you can say calorie."

Every year, the same procedure and the same results. Wasn't that what Einstein had called insanity? In my mind, dieting and teaching were a mismatch made in hell. I was a walker, not a sitter. The kids had to be kept on their toes, never knowing where I would be in three seconds. This teaching business required muscle as well as brain power. Exercise books did not fly to our houses as if by magic or by drones. They had to be carried. Daily. A serf, I contemplated, could not just look at a yoghurt and call it breakfast. It simply was not happening.

"How are you not dead yet, Andrew?" I asked him because I did not understand it.

"Yes, Andrew, what undisclosed information do we not have access to?"

"It's all in the mind, ladies. Conquer your mind, and you conquer your body."

Cara gave him a slap with the datasheet.

"Not eating kills people's spirit, willpower, energy and urge to live. It is a prolonged suicide."

I said to Andrew.

He laughed, and Cara added, " People who diet also turn on the people around them, becoming aggressive, irritable and tired."

"This is accurate. My class had become victims of our teacher's dieting project. Once my Russian teacher had discovered dieting, she halved in size, but the amount of shouting at us doubled. Those were not fun times. Trust me."

I finally looked at the behaviour data for the year group. I wanted to send half the group to this mysterious Mo. Mo should sort them all out. Let them box each other until they are k.o.

"Did you hear how we got banned from the pub up the road?" PE Andrew said.

"No, tell us more,"

"And who are we?" Cara wanted to know.

"Five of us, all from PE, you know, Zaki, Chris, myself, the new girl, I forgot her name, and Suzi. We got a bit unruly, and the bouncer asked us to leave. Suzi, who had more than she could handle, shouted, 'Hey, bouncer, leave us teachers alone.' Like in this song 'Teachers, leave us kids alone." PE Andrew whispered excitedly. Cara's and my head zoomed in closer.

"She just kept singing it really loudly," he explained, "and the bouncer wanted to know where we worked. Oh, my days, I thought we were finished. But Zaki saved us. He told the guy we worked at the 'Achievement and Perfection

Academy'. Then the bouncer said he would contact the school and that we were banned from returning."

"You guys are mad. You know there is CCTV everywhere."

"Come on, Cara, relax. They do not have time for this. Also, the bouncer looked like he believed it. We just got out there very quickly."

PE Andrew was proud of having gotten out of this mess and, simultaneously, having blamed the rival academy. Those PE guys were a fun bunch. Still, I needed more energy for their excitement, weekend trips away and motivational speeches before 8 am.

"Well, you need to find a new pub. They may have your wanted posters up."

"What wanted posters," a voice behind me asked.

"Not wanted posters, wanted students. Students wanted to take this anti-aggression class. We were thinking about Ahmed and Julia. They seem to play up in our lessons quite a bit." Cara stated innocently, and with big puppy eyes, she looked up at Miss Slump, who had positioned herself just behind me.

"Yes, some of the others also suggested both students. Thank you for your input."

We were trying not to laugh. It was easier for me because I had my back turned towards Miss Slump, but Cara and Andrew struggled not to burst.

Once Miss Slump had completed her little tour around the room and taken note of the suggested names, she moved on to the next topic.

"Some of you might have heard about the Kofi incident today."

"Oh dear," Cara whispered," what did he do now?"

As a learning mentor, it was part of her job to liaise with teachers, social workers and educational psychologists. She had to make home visits and speak with parents or carers. Some of the kids Cara worked with had family issues or mental health problems. Cara was an asset to our factory. She had scared me when I first met her. I was unsure whether this tiny woman liked or hated kids or any human. Still, over time, it became clear that she deeply cared for the kids she worked with and knew their families well. Cara had become what her name meant: a friend.

"This morning in his science lesson," Miss Slump explained, "Kofi cut Sarah's hair by around two inches. He just held her by the ponytail and cut her hair."

Oh dear. This was today's crime review. PE Andrew smirked and, with finger scissors, cut the air. Cara and I tried not to laugh at this, behaving increasingly like disorderly kids in class.

"Someone, call the police." He said as quietly as possible. Cara nodded and smiled.

Because Kofi had cut Sarah's hair, an incident report needed to be written, a sanction had to be thought up, and the parents had to be called. Both Sarah's and Kofi's parents. Poor, perfect Sarah, who quietly did all her work and who had the most uplifting smile. She had become the victim of this unfortunate hair incident.

"Kofi's parents should have a direct line installed at their house," Cara quietly suggested, "Like the red bat phone in Gotham City. They get a phone call most days. This boy is a serial offender on the verge of being kicked out."

I tried not to react. Instead, I took my pen with the pink fluffy unicorn at the end of it, opened my planner in the back and scribbled that installing a direct line would be a waste of money because all those phone calls have not made a difference so far and probably won't ever. Without moving her eyes, Cara, with a slight twitch of her lips and pretending she was looking at Miss Slump, read the note, and her thumb went up.

Scribbling notes in meetings was common practice. The clock would be watched, notes exchanged, or messages sent under desks and across the room. The younger serfs used their phones, but Cara and I were old school.

The Kofi incident was the central issue of the afternoon. What followed were reminders for general admin tasks that had to be completed soon. All of this could easily have been an email. I stared at the clock across the room on the light blue wall above the whiteboard. The hands did not move fast enough. The others around me engaged in conversation, contributing to the meeting, but I just wanted to be silent.

I had not had a haircut in ages. There was no time for this when books needed to be marked in different colours and each lesson prepared for at least three different ability levels. Could I hire Kofi? That would be child labour and illegal. Having heard the stories about Sarah's hair in the last 30 minutes, I cancelled my imaginary hair appointment with coiffeur Kofi.

Who would get up first? I scanned the room. Most serfs felt obliged to stay beyond their contracted hours or directed time, as it was called in education speak. They were used to handing out freebies to society. And they did not want to create the impression of being work-shy, although this was what society thought anyway. In the popular imagination, serfs started at 9 am and went home by 3 pm. This trash-talking of our profession was why I had stopped giving to charity years ago. I provided free education every academic year. I came to this realisation around two years ago, after I had completed my calculations. Every week, in pink ink on white paper for the whole academic year, I had recorded all my work, whether it had taken place in the factory, at home, on planes, at Bella's gymnastics competitions, on trains and in queues. I had used my numeracy skills, which I had to prove to the authorities, along with literacy and ICT skills, before even being allowed to become a serf, to work out how many hours I had donated to youngsters. And therefore to the education system and, by extension, the taxpayer. I would have earned another half a year's salary if those hours had been converted into hard cash. But this cash flow had never materialised. I considered the extra hours a form of forced volunteering.

Stanley also stared at the clock. It was time. And, yes, there was movement. At 5 pm on the dot, Stanley stood up, as he did every week.

"Have to pick up the kids," he announced.

No matter the meeting, Stanley could be relied upon. He was the 5 o'clock man. I had not seen this kind of assertiveness in other factories where I had worked. The audacity to stick to agreed times. Someone standing up in a meeting that had yet to be wrapped up by whoever was leading it. Some would call it work to rule or quiet quitting, but after meeting Stanley, I called it setting boundaries. The overlords did not wish to see it for fear of such behaviour catching on, especially with the new generation of serfs who needed to be brought in line before they had completed their two-year indoctrination period.

This constant fiddling in the margins of employment legality had drained many of us to the point of joining unions. Too numerous were the demands made and too frail the reward offered. It helped that Stanley was an active union member, involved father and loving husband. He had other things to do. There was a life worth living outside the factory waiting for him to participate. Some people wanted some Stanley time, too. And he enjoyed time with them.

The first time I had watched Stanley get up, I felt amazed and liberated. That was when I decided I would join this man every time in the combat zone of timekeeping. I even started to plot that I would keep up this 'have to pick up the kids' line until I retired. Bella would be living away, maybe with her own kids, but nobody would know I had no one to pick up in 2050. Nobody! Science allowed people to have kids much later, so nobody would question it. It would be deemed intrusive to ask questions about my age. I could claim emotional trauma, pretend to be offended and cause a big fuss. Being offended was en vogue. However, being offended was a consequence of bumping into other humans. I had a plan, and I would execute it. Until retirement, I would leave at 5 pm every Monday. Come what may.

I admired Stanley for his confidence and assertiveness, something I had to train myself to develop and apply. As a single parent, I needed the cash from the job. The babyfather could have been more charitable. Apart from a single visit every six or seven weeks that lasted a few hours, he did not contribute to Bella's upbringing. He was absent financially as well as emotionally. Thus, I often did work I disagreed with, completed tasks above my pay scale and bit my tongue to keep this job. Like other serfs, I engaged in work that was not part of my contract or responsibilities because I did not want to rock the boat too often. There were ways to get rid of the troublesome serfs. I had seen it and did not want to be in the firing line. Being a serf non grata was not a role I wanted to volunteer for, but I had found ways to arrange myself within the vampire system.

Stanley and I got up and walked out, hearing the rest of the teachers following us. We were leaders of the herd, and the pack was moving. Miss Slump, out of breath, tried to catch up with us. In her Birkenstocks, she wobbled after us, handing us a form to fill in during tomorrow morning's form time. We took it, not even glancing at it. Another piece of paper, another meaningless task.

Stanley looked worried.

"I have not finished the syllabus yet. Why is it exam season already?" He said, "I have no idea how the kids will cope with gross national income, birth and death rates, infant mortality, life expectancy, literacy rates, access to safe water and the Human Development Index?"

"I know, over half the kids in our exam factory are on free school meals. This is their real-life index."

"Exactly, some of the parents work three jobs," Stanley shook his head, "how are they meant to support their kids' revision? Terrible times."

We arrived at the green staffroom door.

Stanley sighed, "See you tomorrow, Eva. Don't work too late."

"You too."

I knew we would both work too much and rest too little. Stanley's blue eyes would not be shut much tonight, nor would they see a movie. Weimar Republic movies were his passion. If anyone only asked a question about them, they would hear an answer that would get thousands of clicks on a YouTube geek channel. Stanley would sit down tonight and work when regular grown-ups watched their favourite TV shows, chatted to their partners, had a beer, and went to the gym or cinema. Stanley would think of ways to help kids understand and remember the ins and outs of economic and social development measures.

Strangers walking along the corridors could almost be fooled into thinking that the exam factory was one of those old, prestigious establishments. The main building was architecturally pretty, not yet Harry Potter style, but pretty and commanding. I, however, had been put into one of the outbuildings that looked more like accommodation for builders and less like Harry Potter Academy. Nobody got to these outbuildings from the outside because they would have ruined the image. They were hidden like secrets, along with the statistics on bullying. I opened the door that led out to the playground and the sports field to walk the two minutes over to my classroom. Still, just as I was about to enter the fresh evening air, I spotted Carlos.

With a big smile, his white teeth beaming, and with his lovely Brazilian accent, he asked, "Hello Miss Eva, how are you?"

"Great to see you, Carlos. I am fine, thank you, and how are you? How is Pedro? Can he walk yet?"

"Soon, he is already holding onto the sofa. I'll

show you."

Carlos leaned the wooden plank he had carried against the shoeprint-stained wall. He got his phone out of the back pocket of his jeans. Carlos was so proud of his little grandson. It showed in the way he admiringly talked about him. He had new photos on his phone every time I bumped into him.

There was little Pedro with his big brown eyes, in green shorts and a yellow dinosaur t-shirt, wobbling along the sofa, falling and getting up repeatedly, whilst his parents in excited Portuguese cheered him on. Twenty-five pounds of uninterrupted cuteness. What a sweet video, I mused. It was good for Carlos that we lived in a time that allowed us to send videos worldwide and keep in touch with family members no matter where they were.

Carlos had left Brazil as a young man over 40 years ago to come to England and marry Laura, whom he had met when she had travelled to Manaus to work in a nursery for a few years. One night, they met in a bar, and that was it. They had been in love ever since. They went back and forth between England and Brazil for the first few years of their marriage until they settled here 25 years ago. Their daughter Laetitia had decided to return to Brazil to study. And just like her mother, she met a man and got married. This is why and how little Pedro with brown curly locks had taken over the most significant part of Carlos' phone storage and heart.

"Wow, look at his chubby legs. He is delightful."

Carlos' grin grew wider and wider. He was a proud grandpa. I wished for him and Laura to be united with their family, not just via technology but for real, with hugs and kisses.

"How is Bella? Are you going to the pool tonight?"

"Yes, I will just get some books and then get Bella. Have a wonderful evening, and please say hello to Laura."

I felt thankful for the human interaction that did not include teaching or education. These invisible fairies, like Carlos, the caretakers, cleaners, IT people, dinner ladies and support staff, oiled the machine's wheels. The overlooked and underpaid.

I switched on the lights, grabbed my bag that said "Better late than ugly," and carried off 30 exercise books. In the car park, other serfs moved towards their cars like robots that needed charging. Their eyes asked *Where is my bed?* And their bodies crumbled under the weight of bags or suitcases carrying exercise books. I went from the factory to Bella's After School Club in my little green Corsa with the wobbly side mirror and the scratched boot door.

Some Year 10 kids waved by the gate, shouting, "Miss, where did you get this car from? The Middle Ages?"

I smiled,d thinking that a car was something I needed to get from A to B in the little time I had. A car did not need to be fancy but functional. If it came in a lovely colour, that was a bonus. Those kids, especially the teenage boys, often laughed at my car.

I passed them slowly and answered, "Had you paid attention in my lessons, you would know that people travelled by horse or walked in *the olden days*."

"Miss, school is over. Stop preaching."

"Never."

In the future, as some of those history-ignoring fun machines had told me weeks ago, they would drive a BMW or a Mercedes. Excellent German cars, quality cars. Good luck to those boys who were quickly impressed by their cousin's security job in the local supermarket, which paid £10.42 per hour and, according to them, required no GCSEs or any other qualifications. I forgave them for their uncritical acceptance of whatever their older cousin had told them about money. Now and then, however, the truth could not be left unsaid, and I changed my lesson to educate the next generation on financial skills. This included a list of all the monthly bills a grown-up had to pay compared to the average monthly wage. It was not part of the official curriculum, but real life was essential. Many kids were shocked into silence. Some started working harder. The most surprised group were the future BMW or Mercedes owners. The dream car needed to be earned and financed. It would not just drive up the road one day, at least not in the type of factory I worked at. The ignorance of the young amused me, but it was worrying, too.

Competing against the glamour of sunny beaches and never-ending holidays was hard for any exam factory. Social media was blessed with contributions by rich nonentities. The ones that were often referred to as celebrities. Celebrity from Latin *celebritās* means *fame* or *the state of being busy or crowded*. Famous, crowded too, but what exactly were they engaged with? Feeding and maintaining their vast attention deficits and egos. Who got to join the celebrity club? Which educational pathway led to fame? Those were the questions I wanted to see answered every time some kid started to tell me admiringly about some influencer.

I had figured out a few ways to stardom but had yet to try them myself. If someone were talented at singing, acting or some high-profile sport, that could work in their favour. Singing or acting would work better. With sports, it had to be the right sport. Football was a money-making machine, as were tennis and boxing to some extent. The problem with tennis was the prior investment. One needed help to turn up somewhere and play. Those rackets were costly, not to mention the fee to book a court. And the outfit, too, required remortgaging. Lack of talent could easily be compensated with a high score in the looks department. The very brave could also try moving into a house with strangers for total exposure on every level, behaving as outrageously as possible whilst wearing as little as possible. Others successfully used the gaming, vlogging, Instagram, or TikTok pathways. Zero-talent people did not have to despair. If they were up for sexual intercourse with an established celebrity, even they could be a winner. Financial success would be instant and guaranteed if that celebrity was already married.

A GCSE in history or an A-level in politics looked less appealing. It meant repetition, revision and honest work. To manage these expectations of, on the one hand, getting away with doing very little as an influencer and, on the other hand, studying for qualification was a tricky balancing act for the serfs in the factories.

Today's problem was that thanks to social media, these people appeared everywhere, or maybe there were just too many self-promoters out there. The contribution by some who challenged politicians to do their jobs was, of course, commendable, but most did not do that. Most wanted to make money out of the general public. Celebrity-inspired products jaundiced me. Additional cooking and baking advice was filmed in kitchens that resembled banquet halls presented by people who had last eaten in 1066. Autobiographies written by people who had left school three minutes before signing the book deal. Workouts were delivered by people who had just returned from their yearly reconstruction treatment in Turkey. The desperate ones invited people to their dating and mating activities, showing off their pregnancies five minutes after conception with a baby shower. This was followed by a gender reveal, which these days was nonsensical. A post-pregnancy glamour shoot cashed more money once the new celebrity entered the world. Finally, it all ended in a high-profile divorce for which those people paid their lawyers six times the average couple earned in a year. They had no shame and exposed their psycho-dramas for all of us to witness and partake. A sane person would keep most of this private, but maybe that was why we were poor and they were rich. Some celebrities wanted to remind everyone that they had donated vast sums of money in a fit of generosity to whatever cause was trendy. Society was expected to clap because it was challenging to give away £20,000 when one was a multimillionaire with an accountant who would cleverly and legally store the rest of the lightly earned money in tax havens.

MONDAY, 5:30 PM

My head was spinning when I stopped next to the rusty fence of the nursery that also ran the Breakfast and After School Club for the primary school next door, which Bella attended.

"Baby Bella, Hello!"

I shouted across the fence, like a mad person. Impatiently, hopping from one leg to

the other, waiting to be let in. Security was paramount, even though this area did not qualify as a Wild West climate. I stood there waiting, wondering how Bella used to go to a continental European nursery where anyone could have just walked into a building and kids did not get kidnapped. Such places would be shut down on this island. This was Alcatraz. The surveillance society had to train their kids early. There she was, the lady with the keys to the children's storage facility. Mrs Shah, the nursery manager, opened the door to the one-story building, smiling kindly.

"Mama, Mama."

Bella’s powerful jump nearly pushed me over.

"Are we going to the pool?" she asked ecstatically.

"Baby, it's Monday. Where else would we go on a Monday evening?"

I felt content. Bella had an incredible day. Ever since she had been to nursery without prison-style security, I could judge from how Bella’s hair and clothes looked at the end of the day whether this had been an enjoyable day for my baby. Bella’s white shirt was no longer tucked into the grey skirt, and her long brown hair had come undone. The neat plait I had created this morning just after breakfast had loosened, and the red bow had entirely disappeared. Bella's tiny fingers were ink-stained. This Monday had been a great day, and now it would get even better because my little mermaid would go swimming.

The drive to the swimming pool was short, but the time needed to be used wisely. The radio was turned off, and the GCSE history textbook on civil rights in America came out.

"Bella, please go to page 23 and read the passage on Martin Luther King for me. Can you see where it says Martin Luther King? Please read from there. Thank you, baby."

Bella obliged. She was used to reading textbook pages aloud for me. There needed to be more hours to tick all the inspection boxes, meet the criteria from the school improvement plan and deliver outstanding lessons. Bella learnt about non-violent protest and bus boycotts, and I pondered how the misery of black Americans could be turned into what the inspectors would consider engaging and imaginative teaching whilst catering for different learning styles and, at the same time, promoting fundamental British values. It's a piece of cake. By the time we had moved on to Malcolm X, Bella and I had arrived at the leisure centre. I had a vague idea for this one lesson but also a slight panic because this was just one of many lessons I still had to prepare for this week.

The middle-aged auburn-haired lady just opposite was trying to manoeuvre her Chelsea tractor into a gap too small for my little Corsa. Why did people have cars like this in a regular English town? This was not a sandstorm-prone area, nor was it Iceland. Also, it was highly unlikely that this lady was on a mission for the Royal Geographical Society. Most females here, I predicted, were in the area to take their kids to some activity for an hour of peace. Nobody hereabouts had to escape from lions or elephants. Their excuse may have been the number of unfixed potholes that could be found, but this was a lame excuse, on the same level as the dog eating my homework.

"Mama, what are we waiting for?"

"I am watching the lady opposite try to park her SUV."

"SUV, what is this?" Bella asked whilst shuffling into the middle of the back seat to have a better view.

The name SUV was stupid. It sounded like a particular unit in the FBI, but it certainly was not. I was not a car pro. Mainly, I judged cars as I judged dresses by colour and affordability.

"SUV, I am not sure, but I think it means something like a sports utility vehicle. Apparently, it is very good to drive on but also off the road."

"Off the road, how? Mami? On the pavement?"

"I think they are not meant to be on the pavement here in England. Maybe this is a good car for people on safari or in the mountains."

"But there is no safari here."

Bella was as annoyed as I was, and we exited the car. Off-road, when they parked so close to a sensible-sized car that nobody could open the door any longer? Off-road, as in getting the little angels to a factory five minutes away from home? Where was the need for those cars? What could those cars do that a normal car could not? Could they fly, cook or entertain kids?

"Do you think we should get a car like this? Or maybe even a tank. What do you think Bella?"

In surveys, drivers of SUVs had stated that safety was their main reason for buying such monstrosities. Theirs, of course. Sadly, statistics told stories of kids being terribly injured by those cars. Unsure of handling the spaceship, some drivers could not get into parking spaces or stay in their lane.

Bella laughed, "A tank, Mami, let's buy a tank."

"Yes, Bella, we go to the tank shop. Your grandpa learnt to drive a Russian tank before he had a driving licence."

But those were the days of the Cold War, with imminent attacks from the Western imperialists possible at any time. Realities were framed to make them fit priorities. People had to be prepared, driver's licence or not. The enemy had to be beaten, and tanks were one way of doing so, or at least so the apparatchik thought.

"Wow?"

"Yes, ask him in two weeks when you are on holiday with him."

"He can teach me."

Bella was excited about the tank. We grabbed our swimming bags from the boot, and by now, the SUV lady had given up and parked elsewhere. She jumped out of her oversized and overrated vehicle, followed by her son, who was a few years younger than Bella. The mum looked like she needed a booster seat. With her, *I buy designer but try to look second-hand look*, she gave the impression of cooking hippie-style vegan food free from whatever tasty ingredient she considered dangerous to ensure her little darling was getting his organic dose of vitamins. In a few years, that little darling would probably turn into a sulky adolescent who demanded to be picked up from some fast food chain restaurant, threatening her with a public anxiety attack should she refuse to chauffeur him around in the wrong type of car.

"Let's go swimming, baby!"
"Yes, and let's dance."

We followed the SUV lady and her son into the leisure centre with our funny dance accompanied by weird animal noises that alarmed others but not anyone who knew us. It had become a tradition to move to the leisure centre in a somewhat odd way. Being different was normal for us. We had fun pretending to be animals or other creatures.

Inside the lifeless changing rooms that reminded me of hospital wards, we squeezed together into one changing booth and got changed, pushing our bellies out and continuing to dance. Bella's polka dot bathing suit was on her body in a flash. She eagerly walked towards the pool. The type of fast walk people put on when they want to run but restrain themselves. That was how Bella edged closer to the water.

I followed slowly, taking my time. Here I was, a practising member of the leisure class. Nothing would make me rush or run or hurry in any way. Running burnt calories, and I was hungry. The cold water on my toes, feet and legs eventually forced me to take a break before counting to three and fully emerging in the water.

I must have been around five or six years old, still in Kindergarten, when my parents had signed me up for swimming lessons. The swimming coaches just threw the kids into the deep end. There were no child-centred activities like going into the kids' pool first, getting used to water or doing little fun things in the water. None of this had existed. It was sink or swim, literally. And I sank, and so the coach, as was typical, slowly walked over holding some long metal stick with a ring the size of a medium-sized cooking pot at the end of it. To this device I was meant to hold on to, and I did, in fear for my life. Neither coaches nor parents thought this was unusual or cruel. Most kids had learnt to swim like this. But on this day, I decided that I did not need another assignment in waterboarding. I hated it and was too scared to return to the lesson. In fact, I was too scared to go back to any pool. A week later, when it was time for the next lesson, I refused. I could still see vividly in front of my eyes how my mum tried to drag me away from the armchair and how I clung to the red armchair in the living room, screaming and kicking. It must have looked cartoonish. I did not let go. I was strong when I wanted to be. Nobody would throw me into the deep end again.

Bella knew how to swim, having had successful, more kid-friendly lessons a few years earlier when we had lived on the continent across the Channel. I had little to worry about in the pool. The lanes clearly indicated whether one was meant to swim slowly or fast, and Bella and I chose to swim slowly. I loved this time in the pool. I did not need to talk but could watch people and think. Those were things I enjoyed. Two lanes down, wannabe Michael Phelps-type swimmers were huffing and puffing, eye-rolling anyone swimming at a reasonable speed. Those who slowed them down and messed around with their target times were enemies and needed to know their place, which was the slow lane. For them, this swimming thing was serious business. Those people were the same people who had gone into a diet frenzy because summer was nearing. They only had a light dinner, meaning a carrot waved over parmesan. Sprinkled with melon seeds for the aroma. The type of people with a lack of problems created some and expected the rest of us to validate them, just like those who attended these boot camps that had jumped up every Saturday morning in the parks around our local area. Walking and enjoying nature was impossible because a military drill sergeant shouted and screamed at a middle-aged crowd in lycra breathing heavily. They had paid to be shamed, degraded and embarrassed into fat-burning activities. If this happened to a child, social services would be called, yet grown-ups made the conscious choice to let it happen to them. Money went down the drain as far as I was concerned. By Christmas, the yoyo effect had caught up with pre-diet times. Those people's suspended logic led the weight-loss industry to continuous profits as the clowns turned up to join the circus on an annual subscription.

Yet, it was not surprising given today's culture, driven by influencers and self-promoters who endorse restriction belts around people's bodies. Dieting and body alterations mastered their boredom. They filtered out their natural curves. They hired nutritionists, personal trainers and chefs to look like they had no food access. I disagreed with those folk and their monkish asceticism, just like I disagreed with the never-ending personal target setting. I said no to that. My curves were an investment in safety and happiness. Heavy people did not get kidnapped. It made sense. A kidnapper wanted to make money. They did not want to spend it on food to keep their victim alive waiting for the ransom. Ladies attracted potential partners via their curves. It was evolution. A skinny chef did not look legit. They could not be trusted. The higher a person's BMI, the more likely their friends would enjoy coming to their house, knowing there would be proper food, not those light or calorie-reduced, taste bud-killing bites, but real munchies. I refused to hand my money to the industry and made everyone grumpy. Those mind twisters would buy themselves a mansion from the cash people threw away for diet products. They did not do this because they cared. They wanted to build a kitchen extension, so they convinced others to avoid eating. And then they could eat more and better. I wanted nothing to do with the smoothie police or hang out with the white egg omelette squad because I loved to indulge in high-calorie food.

The non-descript lifeguard on the other side of the pool underneath the huge station clock was alert and scanned the pool. Not exactly the type of lifeguard I remembered from the Baywatch TV show that had been hugely popular with my generation. He had clearly not signed up for Saturday morning boot camp but probably knew how to save someone. Health and safety was not to be underestimated. Half an hour into the water session, Bella went to the kids' pool to dive in shallow water. She was pretending to be like Ariel the Little Mermaid, a movie I had to watch a thousand times with Bella. Occasionally, she would excitedly wave to indicate for me to watch her new moves. The new moves were not new but had to be applauded and smiled at anyway. Kids loved to share their skills repeatedly, and parents were obliged to be always excited. The joys of parenting.

After some time, I joined Bella in the small pool and watched her perform the little stunts close up, counting how many seconds she could dive and how many seconds she could do a handstand. I knew Bella would sleep well because the water had a sleeping pill effect on her.

"Do you have dragon coins, please?"
"Dragon coins? What are those, baby?"
"The coins for the hair dryer."

I had to smile and handed over a few 20p coins.

"Here you go. They are pretty weak dragons, don't you think?"
"They are very noisy dragons," Bella said, "but not as good as our hair dryer at home."

The leisure centre hair dryers managed to huff and puff microscopic wheezes of warmish air, killing everyone's sense of hearing and turning people in close vicinity into lip readers. Bella skipped over to the rambunctious air puffer, her wet hair dripping onto her white school blouse. My eyes followed her. People would say she was a little girl, but she was also so grown-up and mature, a good girl. Good girls often carried trauma, and I was aware of this. I knew that Bella missed her Abbu, who lived in London and was unlike those other dads who were involved and could be relied upon. Since we had split up just before Bella was two, he took little responsibility. He was more the kind of fun machine dad who showed up hours late and did not really plan anything. Despite being a parental zero, he thought of himself as excellent. Bella never really showed her disappointment and sadness; instead, she smiled and laughed through misery. She wanted the people around her to be happy, even if they repeatedly broke promises and failed her. Bella held no grudges. There was never enough time to give to this good girl.

"I hate you," the boy from the car park shouted, lying on his back, trying to kick his mum, the SUV driver.

"Put your trousers on now and stop screaming."

She was trying to stay calm, but it was not easy. The boy with the enraged eyes had tears rolling over his red, freckled, round face. I felt conflicted. My teacher persona wanted to tell the disorderly bundle on the floor to calm down and somehow distract him. My parent persona wanted to hug the mum. My zombie persona wanted to make the mum and kid disappear. I gathered together our things and grabbed both bags.

"Come on, Bella, let's go." With a gentle smile for the exhausted SUV mum and her offspring, I pushed the dirty changing room door open with my shoulder because public facility doors distributed hurricanes of bacteria and germs. Bella slipped out quickly, and we danced back to the car together. This dance was slower and would have gained fewer marks than the one we did earlier, but that was okay because it was late, and we both needed calorific energy.

"Can we have McDonald's tonight?" Bella inquired.

Her eyes were wide open, and she had a giant clown smile on her face, fastening her seat belt. She already knew the answer.

"I suppose we won't have time to cook tonight."

It was standard procedure after a day like this one. Everyone's favourite family restaurant was just opposite the leisure centre. What an ideal location. Genius. I was a sucker for cheeseburgers and fries. A habit with staying power.

"It will take us at least one minute to drive there, baby. Do you think you can manage?"

"I can."

No matter where I had taken Bella, the cheeseburgers and fries in McDonald's tasted the same around Europe. It was one of our favourite places to have food. I sometimes dreamt of a guy taking me to McDonald's and smuggling champagne. What could be a better date? Like Italian restaurants, McDonald's was a quality place to get fed. Too many people trash-talked McDonald's, especially those helicopter parents, self-appointed healthy eating enforcers, whose kids were not allowed near fast food places. But this hardcore militancy against cheeseburgers was not justified. There had been a study by a German consumer organisation that had rated several burger chains, and they had found that McDonald's cheeseburgers were good quality. Truth tellers!

My parking was not too great but not as bad as the SUV mum's parking. At least I could apply my spatial awareness to determine whether my car fit into a gap. In fact, I probably thought more often than not that my car was a bit more oversized than it actually was. Equally, a mirror breaking off here or there was just a side effect of driving, not the end of the world. If everyone bought a second-hand car, society could relax more because scratches would matter less. The handbrake pulled up, and the seat belt was undone. We sang the McDonald's song from the ad because *we were loving it.*

This McDonald's was special. It had a security guard, like a nightclub. How exciting, as if we were partying on a school night. A cute girl and a beautiful mother had no problems getting past security guys. This guard was not here for us. He was here as part of the damage control programme. We did not give the impression of wanting to damage anything, nor did we need controlling.

More often than not, McDonald's branches in the area had become the unofficial social clubs for teens. Although they might have bought some food, they did not follow the carefully masterminded idea of fast food establishments: to eat as quickly as possible on uncomfortable seats and leave until returning another time to spend more money. In the eyes of the management, those youngsters overstayed their welcome by slouching on the seats and benches, acting unruly, and developing the unfortunate tendency to intimidate others. This led to big, scary-looking, probably harmless men being employed to look tough at entrances. Security appeared in most restaurants over the last few years, just like the police had in educational establishments.

Bella was drawn to the Happy Meal but decided the toy was too babyish, and she would just have chicken selects and fries instead. I added my mandatory two cheeseburgers and fries and two orange juices as vitamins were vital. Having paid, we sat down and munched on our quality dinner, watching other customers around us, mostly teenagers. This place did not attract the elderly.

" Ali had to go to the Head of Year. That must have been so scary. Can you imagine it?"

"Why would it have been scary to go to the Head of Year? What makes you think the Head of Year was scary?"

"Mami, have you ever heard them shout? They shout so much. Sometimes, when they shout, I want to cover my ears, and my hair feels like flying, like in the Bollywood movies I watch with Abbu sometimes." Bella gestured with her hands, full of chicken and fries, close to her ears to visualise the noise level.

"I know, baby, I know. I have heard it too. Sometimes they shout," I agreed, "but baby, I will tell you something. A Head of Year is just a grown-up who works at school. I do not want you to be scared of them. They are no different from any other grown-ups. If you ever have to go to the Head of Year, just be yourself. Be kind and polite, and they will probably be nice too. Ok?"

"Hm, I hope so."

Bella was not convinced. I was disappointed in a factory system that induced weapons-grade anxiety in their youngsters. A system where 8-year-olds were scared of a Head of Year, someone they should be able to trust. What a disturbed world.

"When I am big, I want to work in McDonald's."

"Wow, I will visit you at work every day." I laughed.

"Do you think McDonald's people get lots of money?"

"I don't know, baby, probably okayish money. I want to know whether they get free food?"

"Mami, you would work here if there were free food."

We both giggled.

If free food was available, Bella was right; I could be tempted into considering a career change, but only after the teach-in-prison option. No lesson planning or, in this case, recipe planning is required. Just turning up at work without having to prepare materials in several languages and for different ability levels. That could be heaven, and just going home without marking papers and exercise books after work sounded good to me.

But most people probably imagined that

their job was harder than someone else's. Did those workers belong to the group of workers checked up on by cameras and had their toilet break times recorded and deducted from their real break times? Who knew what totalitarian surveillance practices were used on them? Maybe none, maybe more Orwellian ones. In places such as McDonald's, an added problem was the customer. Hell, indeed was, other people.

To the sound of Green Day blasting, we arrived opposite our ground floor flat in the two-storey house on the outskirts of the town. Elizabeth, our Helen Mirren look-alike neighbour, just moved her recycling bin into the correct spot for tomorrow morning's collection.

"How are you both?"

"Great, thank you. We have been swimming and had dinner at McDonald's," said Bella.

"Good to see you, Elizabeth, I would have forgotten that the recycling bins were due tomorrow. How are you?"

"I am well, Eva. I am looking forward to July. The kids and grandkids are flying in from Dubai, and we are planning a trip to Cornwall."

"Wow, that sounds fantastic. Well, we better go in. It's Bella's bedtime, and I have marking to do."

"Sure, no worries. Good night, Bella."

Elizabeth would understand I had no time

for an extended chat. As a mother of two, she knew the importance of bedtime; as a mother of a teacher, she understood marking and preparation. That was precisely why her daughter and her son-in-law had left for Dubai. The drudgery at home had become unbearable, and Dubai offered similar money, better weather and a lighter workload, so overall, it was an upgrade.

Good for them, I thought. One day, this is what I would do too: leave for a better place, but right now, Bella was to be near her dad. I had to provide him with at least the opportunity to prove he was a good dad, even though he chose to hide it. As Norman Cousin once said, *hope is independent from the apparatus of logic.* And this was true because when I applied logic and reasoning to Bella's dad, it was clear that there would never be a change. For Bella, I hoped that I was wrong. Finding my keys at the bottom of my bag, I opened the door. Bella skipped into the flat we rented, threw her swimming bag next to the sofa and jumped right onto it, legs and arms stretched out.

"I am tired."

"Me too, baby. Please get ready for bed, and remember we brush our teeth for three minutes, not three seconds."

"Okay, okay, I know this."

"Last time we used the blue plaque-revealing

tablets, your teeth looked pretty blue. Do you recall?"

Bella turned around, grinning like a shark ready to bite, nodding. I quickly took the recycling out and moved the bin closer to the road next to Elizabeth's. It was getting darker. Most bins had been neatly lined up, ready for collection. I thought about how kids would go to bed along this road, tucked in by their parents and how couples would sit down to relax. I had an appetite to binge on crime shows and switch off, but not today. There was still too much to prepare for tomorrow.

MONDAY, 8:25 PM

The yellow curtains in Bella's room, with the big monkeys, had been drawn, a story had been read, kisses had been blown and caught, and Bella was ready for a good night's sleep. Gone were the days when I had to read Cinderella repeatedly. Even longer gone were the days when I could skip half the story and pretend it was over. Bella paid attention and asked questions about anything we read together. But after swimming, there was hardly any talking. She fell asleep before the story about the witch who lived in a purple house was finished. I was deliberating, walking straight across from Bella's room into my tiny bedroom stuffed with textbooks and a small wardrobe full of colourful second-hand charity shop dresses. Money was better spent on travelling rather than fashion. Instead, I took myself downstairs and did what I did most nights. I got my white mug that said *#tired - I woke up like this*, a gift from Alisha, a former student, and made myself a builder's tea.

Waiting for the teabag to turn my mug into a

brown brew, I looked at the corner by the door. On the ugly green carpet with scraps of wood from the wall, just next to the radiator, was the heavy bag containing a pile of year 11 exercise books. The bag stared at me. It stood by the shoe rack like a jailor who had just instructed the jailed, waiting for them to comply. I did. I complied. But first, I hung up the swimming clothes and towels and threw the tea bag in the bin. I grabbed the 30 books and sat at the table in the open-plan kitchen- the living room next to the fridge, which always hummed.

Josie, an ex-colleague, came up with the phrase, *boyfriend shift* to describe the late-night sessions because most people would hang out with a friend, boyfriend, girlfriend or partner at this hour, but teachers hung out with their books and with marking. This night shift, which should have been spent on someone or something relaxing and fun, was now forever the boyfriend shift. The pile had to be completed before the overlords started their book-look tomorrow around lunchtime.

The book look, work scrutiny or any other fancy name was given to check whether we serfs had marked and corrected the exercise books following the factory's guidelines. Unreal, sky-high expectations of the inspectors were dreaded and resented nationwide. I opened the first book, quickly glancing over every page since I had last marked them two weeks ago.

Where were my green pens? Not the red ones. No, no, no. They could damage and harm kids psychologically. Too aggressive, too in their face, too negative. Generations over generations across the world have suffered some severe PTSD because of red teacher marking. Red was threatening youngsters, and the education system would produce a new generation of mental asylum detainees or prisoners if red were used. Surely, I did not want this. Instead, I had to feed into this junk science thought up in a group-think session and obliged. Green it was. Positive and fresh. Green, a new beginning. Fabulous!

I thanked all those kids who had been excluded or had damaged their attendance records by being at home for the day. They did not require marking in green. What lovely creatures they were. They gave me a bit of a break. Their physical absence had prevented them from producing any work. A beautiful sight when marking! Less was more. But, the ones whose mental absence, commonly known as laziness, had prevented them from doing what they were meant to do during the lesson were a real problem, like Hoodie Boy. His and other kids' withdrawal caused me to panic. I was forced to engage in lengthy dialogue on paper. Commenting on what was not there and should have been on paper, why it was not there, and how it could be there. Even though this dialogue, or rather monologue because those kids did not answer meaningfully, had already taken place in the lesson, I now had to write it down again because this lack of work was an indicator of my failure.

It did not matter that Shazia was planning her wedding to her cousin and was not bothered with history. It did not matter that the new boy in the corner, whose name I had forgotten, had declared that schoolwork did not matter because he was only interested in studying his religion. It also did not matter that Tom wanted to be a professional footballer and had only seen the use of education if it was physical education. Those facets did not matter, neither to the overlords nor to the inspectors. I was the troublemaker because I had failed to engage, motivate, and create exciting lessons. Therefore, all this green marking had to be done upbeat. I did not want to put any kid off learning by using negative language in my marking or by stating the obvious, which was that the kid who had not engaged even after having been approached in the lesson several times, even after having had tasks explained and modelled, even after having been asked which part they did not understand. Some kids simply could not be bothered to do what they had been asked. It was my deficient teaching that had sent them to this point. I had to *fix-up*. My failings were there for all to see on those empty pages.

I composed a lovely note for Hoodie Boy.

"Thank you for attending our history lesson. Please have a look at the worksheet over there."

I drew a giant arrow in green towards a worksheet I had just stuck into the book with glue sticks I had bought with my money. A worksheet that had also been handed out in the previous lesson but had been used as a basketball and ended up in the bin. In a pleasant, calm manner, I continued to ask Hoodie Boy to write down which reason he would regard as the most important for America's withdrawal from Vietnam. I politely asked him if he could also explain why he thought this was the most important reason. There was no pressure, of course.

I ended this idiotic exercise with a "Thank you so much". More cynical sarcasm.

What I wanted to write would have gotten me fired, and I needed the money. I was still caught in the stranglehold of a system that blamed the wrong people. Thus, positivity was the flavour of the day. I gave all the kids this positivity because it paid my bills. I was playing along to this madness. When in the circus, be the clown!

But of course, there were those kids who were a pleasure to teach, who came to the factory each day ready to store more knowledge in their spongey brains to be retrieved during the exam period. The ones who shouted *Miss Miss* from across the playground. The ones who waved excitedly when they spotted any teacher. The ones who drew pictures and believed their teacher would cherish those art pieces instead of burying them under PDFs of new initiatives and the latest inspection framework. The ones who came from abroad without English and finished top of the class a few years later. The ones who smiled silently in lessons and nodded when I modelled the essay structure whilst Hoodie Boy kicked over a chair and marched out.

They were lovely, and they were the silent majority. And I knew they had to remain my focus when I wanted to apply at McDonald's or for prison jobs. They had to remain my focus when friends working in private schools told me about the longer holidays, the restaurant-style food and cream-skimmed selected cohorts who were mortified at getting Bs and the school trips to the Far East and America. Those kids who showed up daily and did what they were meant to do deserved good teachers. They deserved Stanley, who would also crouch over his computer right now, having put to bed his two kids and kissed his cancer-stricken wife.

Those kids needed us, but we needed sleep and rest. Those kids could not be collateral damage in the educational warzone.

The length of a blockbuster later, all exercise books were marked. For a short while, I felt relieved, but before long, anxiety set in as I anticipated the same procedure tomorrow evening and the evening after. This would continue until I marked myself into the grave or out of this factory. At one point, I had taught 17 different groups and nearly collapsed under the marking. 90 minutes per set. It should have taken me 17 evenings to mark them all, but the overlords only allowed a gap of 14 days between marking. I had to be creative with my time.

For tonight, I was done. Every book was as green as the hulk. Tomorrow morning, in lesson 2, I would ensure that every kid reads the green feedback mini-essay I had written and replies in a different colour. This was necessary as it had to be evident to a book-look checker that different people were engaged in written dialogue. Everything had to be tamper-proof. Ultimately, if a kid failed to do so, I had to hide their book from the overlords who would question my teaching capability over the inability of a kid to follow a simple instruction. To keep the overlords from blaming me for the student's lack of work, I had to keep an eye on the likes of Hoodie Boy, who was in the business of ignoring instructions, and his book definitely had to disappear into the boot of my 20-year-old car. There, it would stay alongside others until the book look was over, and it was safe to return the evidence of my failings as a teacher. Usually, I did well in book looks. It's probably because I had mastered some tricks in rule bending. Lack of time had led to creativity, just like lack of money had made my grandparents' generation fix cars with nothing and turn into MacGyvers. They had become creative souls because there were few resources to help them fix whatever needed fixing, yet they did it.

I remembered that the civil rights lesson I had planned in the car still needed a PowerPoint with a captivating visual stimulus to direct the students' gaze away from live-streamed PE lessons outside my classroom. I thanked all available gods for the invention of YouTube. Two little clips to introduce both Malcolm X and Martin Luther King were precisely what I needed to start the lesson. A pair work activity followed by a written task embellished with a peer assessment against the criteria from the exam board. And the lesson was done. I quickly created a worksheet for Sana, who had just arrived at the factory four weeks previously, spoke no English and had never been to a school in her life. But here, she was forced to study the civil rights movement when maybe some small group English lessons would have benefitted her more. Thus, I used many pictures and simple English, hoping that the teaching assistant who spoke Sana's language could work with Sana on Martin and Malcolm. Even MLK said that *we must accept finite disappointment but never lose infinite hope*. True words. Perhaps something would stay stuck, and none of this was done in vain. The teaching assistants were angels, lifesavers for kids and teachers. They whizzed around in the background, got some of the most challenging kids to engage in work, took out those who were aggressive, helped them to calm down, spoke several languages and were able to support others who had just arrived from war zones or who had been child soldiers in their short lives.

I knew what it was like to be a teaching assistant. I started my journey in the English education system many years ago in a constantly inspected factory because it was deemed inadequate or special measures as it was labelled back in those days. I had supported kids with behavioural difficulties in an inner-city factory. Once, a father had threatened to beat me up, and the police had to escort me off the premises to ensure I was safe. This was a distressing sociological exercise located near London's most expensive properties where, oddly, most families lived in poverty. It was centred around a mixture of all imaginable social problems, drugs, stabbings, child abuse, and gang violence, in addition to the usual academic and educational challenges. It was here I saw an experienced teacher walk out of a lesson, sit on the floor and cry. This should have acted as a warning to me, but it did not. I still had the regrettable tendency to turn a blind eye to bad situations in which I found myself. I was high on toxic positivity. Years later, I had lost it. I still became a serf, but not before I entered the opposite side of the education universe as a language assistant in a private school. Here, I underwent my education in education and learned this country had no middle ground, nothing to resemble what I considered continental normality. Kids either had a superb education or were lucky to survive school. I decided not to uncritically accept what the inspectors or a factory's website claimed but rather to ask the ordinary serfs, teaching assistants, parents and kids about their typical state of affairs in their exam factory.

My phone flashed. It was the social butterfly Rumi, who worked in media and whom I had known since university.

"Girl, I need to see you. How does Friday sound?"

Rumi was always up for a party, although she had calmed down a few months ago when she started to plan her wedding, which was to take place in Florence. I shivered just thinking about people. I loved being alone. Contacting others might have illuminated Rumi's mood, but not mine.

"Bella has a birthday party. I have to pick her up. Can't make it to London."

This was partially true because Bella had to attend a birthday party but not this Friday. Never mind, Rumi would be unaware of this and would not question a single mum having to take her kid to a party. Maintaining friendships and being a member of the anti-social social club was a balancing act.

"Ah, I miss you."

For a second, I worried whether something was wrong with me for refusing to go out more often than not. Was I suffering from anthropophobia, a fear of people? People with anthropophobia avoided crowds, feared eye contact or worried that they were being judged. It was not possible. I was in crowded places all day, constantly held eye contact and was always judged. It could not be anthropophobia. But were there others out there with an innate desire for solitude? Where were these people?

"Rumi, how about next week? Bella will be in Austria."

"Next Friday, it is. I will send you the details. I

have heard of this new place we need to try."

"It's in the diary."

I hoped this was not another one of those soft openings Rumi liked to take me to. The first time I heard of one of these, I was intrigued by the words *soft opening*. It sounded naughty. It sounded enjoyable. So, without being told what it was and without having researched it beforehand, I went along with Rumi to one such soft opening. And that is when I found out it was when a restaurant opened, or in this case, reopened after the chef, manager, cleaner, or whoever had changed. And, according to Rumi, during the soft opening, food was a bit cheaper. I had noticed why everything was cheaper. It was because the portions were smaller, too. A clever move. This soft opening. It was a big pile of leftover garbage. This nonsense drove me to my pots, recipe books, home-cooked meals or local takeaway places.

I figured that being surrounded by thirty human beings all day; some hardly socialised, others more so, did not help me become more social. Noisy classrooms and over-excited kids had helped me appreciate solitude far more than when I was younger and had experienced FOMO. Those days were long gone and now I could not wait to miss out on social engagements and what other people called fun. Most kids at the factory were also unable to adjust their volume. No wonder that I did not want to see or hear anyone.

How people enjoyed socialising remained an enigma to me. I was curious to know how Rumi was forever out meeting people. I did not mind a glimpse through my front window, followed by a nod towards people I knew but people in my face without some sort of buffer zone after factory hours. That just sounded awful and had to be avoided under most circumstances. I hold a master's degree in social distancing. My inner hermit wanted to stay in my enchanted exile at home or somewhere in Sicily.

I went vertiginous thinking about invitations to various social events that I had gotten over the last fortnight. Instead, solitary pursuits interested me. I was also anxious about all the things that came along with people. Self-correcting behaviours, sanitised speech, wearisome small talk, deciphering facial expressions or avoiding offence. All amid noise. I could no longer adapt to the onslaught of so-called fun. I wanted to be the geek in my parent's basement. Still, now I was the parent, and my parents were far away. They never had a basement, and neither did I.

It was nearly midnight, and I felt exhausted, not from this Monday, which had started 18 hours ago, but from this lack of work-life balance. What was it? Where could I find it?

Sixty hours per week, every week. It was not sustainable until retirement. At 35, I felt 74. The holidays did not help either. The only difference was the commute. The work itself continued. It was never done. Weekends meant work. Half-terms were taken up by illness. Easter and Christmas breaks were used to catch up with what could not be completed last term. Summer holidays were always halved by some dumbass new initiative or change in the curriculum. Nothing was ever finished. Although I was tired, my monkey brain was activated, and I did not find sleep easily.

TUESDAY, 7 AM

I had forgotten to put an empty whiskey bottle in the recycling bin and quickly went outside before the bin was picked up. Elizabeth was already back from her daily walk. She waved and came towards me. We both had a clear view of the lady who lived opposite, with her Porsche-driving investment banker husband and two privately educated kids. They had settled on the lovely, expensive side of the street. She walked away from the recycling bin she had just pushed down her pristine driveway, still in her dressing gown and hair in a beige towel. Rich people do not do colour. She spotted Elizabeth and me and nodded over, and so did we.

"She makes candles."

"What, like in a factory? As a business?" I wanted to know more.

"Yes, she makes candles at home. That's her business, and then she goes to the co-working space down the road and networks."

A few times, I received an email from this co-working place. They were looking for new people to rent some of the spaces available. To appear human, they included a selection of people renting an office there. Each one offered a short bio next to their professional headshot. Their bio, one of those newish personal introductions that had become standard, was an advertisement for oneself. People had to appear super-approachable and fun yet professional and grounded in their zen. It gave strangers a chance to assess someone's coolness factor.

"Ah, I know where it is; they have emailed me, too," I said," What job should I do?"

"I have heard there are clothes consultants, mindset facilitators, card makers and motivational speakers." Elizabeth looked at me over the rim of her glasses.

"Do these jobs make a lot of money? Every career adviser in schools would staple their ears to the wall if a 15-year-old came up with those jobs."

"I have heard that thanks to lack of government funding, there were not many career advisers around anymore," Elizabeth replied, whispering, "You know what I call those jobs? Hubby jobs or hobby jobs. Unnecessary for human survival. The women with rich hubbies can do those hobby or hubby jobs."

We both stood there nodding. Those jobs, hobby jobs or rich hubby jobs did not pay bills. They required a financially stable background disguised as a rich husband, lover or sugar daddy. They were also the sort of jobs that relied on wealthy clientele having too much money to waste on something unnecessary.

"How many candles does she need to sell to afford an office and pay the usual bills, mortgage, council tax, water, gas, electricity, food, school uniforms and fees, clothes, etc.?" I asked.

"An impossible undertaking. Unless, of course, someone else had already taken care of the bills. Sales are optional when sustaining life has already been paid for."

"Must be nice when you do not need to reevaluate your choices to take into account reality. Her reality is money on tap."

"True words. How did people get on with life without a motivational speaker? How was anything ever invented or discovered without them?" Elizabeth wondered.

I knew the answer to this. People just got their act together, got up in the morning and got going. Life happened without those people with fake jobs on a self-finding mission.

I heard Bella shout from the bathroom. "Mami, help."

Her electric toothbrush had dropped to the floor, where it had kept spinning and distributing toothpaste in all directions. Bella's school jumper looked like it had toothpaste glitter all over.

"It looks like you need to change your jumper," I said, laughing, "I will clear this toothpaste mess."

"Mami, this was very funny, like a science experiment."

Wiping the floor, I wondered what type of fake job I could do. None was the answer because I had actual bills to pay, and I was too old for a sugar daddy.

"Mami, music, please."

I had not even noticed how I had driven for three minutes without music. I had been too engrossed in thinking about this lady and her candles. Bella loved singing. It amused me when she screamed out the lyrics to a song, not really understanding what they meant.

"Bella, remember, those songs are for our car only. They are not for school or when you are in Abbu's car."

"I know, I know, Mami. Missy Elliot does not go to school."

"Correct, Missy Elliot is done with school."

Tuesday, 8:10 am

I did not want a lecture about my apparently poor parenting from Bella's factory or dad, even though it was me who kept Bella alive daily with almost no financial and even less practical or emotional support. Having dropped Bella at her breakfast club opposite the primary factory, which furnished Bella's brain, I drove five minutes to my factory, passing some early bird kids and Mike. He was the police officer stationed at my factory. He was nondescript. People hardly noticed him. Mike was just there in the background.

"Eva, let me show you something interesting," he said, "look at this."

"Wow," I stopped breathing briefly, "is this in our factory?"

"Yes. That's what I confiscated last week."

He had shown me a photo of a desk filled with knives and machetes.

"No way," I was slightly shocked, "those gadgets do not look like my kitchen knives. Why do the kids walk around with them? I didn't know there were so many gangsters here."

"They are not all gangster kids. Other people will associate each individual, especially a boy, living in a certain postcode with a certain gang," Mike explained, "It's not really a choice. There is no opt-out box they can tick. That's just the way it is around here."

"It is very scary to know that kids have this in classrooms. I hope they won't use them."

"Don't we all. Have a good day."

I walked into the school thinking that the Lottery of Life handed out unwanted prizes. The postcode decided which team someone was on. As everyone felt scared and threatened, they would carry a weapon, just in case. It was an insane kamikaze mission from which it was difficult to escape. Sad times. Mike waved and smiled. I smiled back, carrying my heavy bag full of hulked-up books. This was my daily exercise; I didn't want to do more lifting. I did not have time to join a gym anyway, so this was it. Lifting something out of the boot was my boot camp.

"Morning Flora, what are you buying today?" I greeted the scary receptionist, who most certainly was not a flower.

"A birthday present for Sullivan's wife," The purple-haired lady with a ring on her nose replied in a deep voice.

"He is too busy to do it himself. It's the same every year. Sometimes I wonder whether I should send her a birthday card since I organise everything. For his kids, too."

"Some men are unbelievable." I walked off.

It was a mission to get past Flora. You would not get in unless you had Flora-approved business to do at the factory. She was the factory's official bouncer. The size of a ten-year-old and with the mouth of a rottweiler, she was not to be underestimated. Nobody wanted to be in her bad books. Flora really did not match the image the factory tried to portray on their website and in their fancy open evening brochures. How did Flora manage to be here? How was she allowed to look the way she looked? What did she have on the overlords? I was intrigued. Several times a day, Flora was by the gate, smoking with some of the learning mentors and serfs who had developed a nicotine habit. I was convinced that Flora had completed the same course in barking at strangers that GP receptionists had to pass before working in a GP's surgery.

I turned right and walked away from the offices of the overlords. They were located to the left of the entrance. I could not get into that area anyway. My keycard did not open the doors to the leadership area. I was a serf and had no business in the centre of power. The overlords knew that buildings defined behaviour. Keeping serfs out by having their keycards programmed so that the doors would simply not open was a way to tell them that, as serfs, they were not welcome in high places. I walked into my little world, the one that meant teaching. In the distance, I made out Carlos fixing some shelves. I wondered whether he had even been home.

TUESDAY, 8:50 AM

The first lesson of the day started with a bang.

"Miss, do you give blow jobs?"

Sunjit figured this question would make the Battle of Britain more interesting.

N*ot on Tuesdays.* I wanted to reply. Instead, I chose to ask Agata, the Polish teaching assistant, to escort the overweight 14-year-old, whose brother resided in Pentonville prison for having run a local Cannabis farm, out of my classroom.

Some of his friends giggled. Others were clueless. I continued teaching as if nothing had happened. I knew the overlords would later frame this as a one-off incident. Sunjit, who was called Ladoo by his friends, a word for Indian sweets or slang for fattie as in this case, pretended to be overly confident to mask his lack of intellect. With his shirt hanging out of his trousers, this youngest boy in a family with five kids followed Agata. He walked slowly because his size did not allow him to walk at an average speed. Sunjit, whom teachers would call an underachiever across the board with surface-level intelligence, believed he could shock me. Those comments, however, did nothing but shock me. They had become part of the job, like marking, meetings and lesson preparation. The Battle of Britain concluded without further interruptions or questions on sexual practices.

I looked forward to my personal planning and preparation time in lesson 3 later. But first, I had to deal with Hoodie Boy and his crew. It was time for them to act and comment on my boyfriend shift from last night.

"Good morning." I put on my enthusiastic smile.

"Hm."

"Good morning."

"Hello."

"Good morning."

No response.

"Good morning."

"Hello, Miss, I like your dress."

"Good morning."

No response.

Once most kids had arrived, I left my greeting post, shut the door behind me quietly and walked up and down each aisle of desks, telling kids in an upbeat voice that their work had been great. They needed to make sure they replied to my comments. I had Good Morning-ed every kid on their way into the classroom. This was a must. Teachers had to stand by the door like Mediterranean waiters outside their restaurants or security guards in high-end shops. It was meant to move kids on quickly from one class to the next, away from the overcrowded corridors or the open savannah that was the playground. As I taught in an outbuilding, kids usually took longer to arrive. There were more places to hide on the way and more opportunities to forget the way on purpose.

The kids had picked up their books when entering the classroom. Equipped with their red pens, they sat at the desk on their blue or grey chairs with chewing gum of all flavours stuck underneath and started. The hidden curriculum had been fully installed in their systems. They would be the future workers who would show up on time and not ask for a pay rise, who, without complaining, would endure ever more ridiculous working conditions. The fallacy of meritocracy had been successful.

Ten minutes into the lesson, Hoodie Boy and two of his underlings appeared in the classroom.

He walked to his seat, nodding my way, asking, "Alright, Miss History?"

This caused an uproar and laughter amongst the rest of the hormonal bunch, but not for too long. Most kids realised that the exams were knocking heavily at the door. It was not enough time, and yet it was too much. There were too many lessons which I had to spend with Hoodie Boy and his escapades. Picking him up on his use of language towards me, would have caused a domino effect of confrontation. I let this one slip.

Gone were the days of study leave that allowed and trusted kids to revise at home. My factory had decided that all the kids benefitted from attending every lesson until the exams. Over the last few weeks, I listened to the high achievers asking for advice on avoiding the factory and getting permission for study leave. There was no way out. I had sympathy for them. They knew that their learning would be disrupted in the factory by the likes of Hoodie Boy. They were forced to spend all day at the factory. Only by 4 p.m., after an exhausting day, would they finally be able to revise peacefully. Bunking was not an option. That would drag their attendance record down. It could see parents fined or, worse, imprisoned like this one mother a few years back whose teenage daughters had failed to attend school. As a result, the mum was imprisoned, and many asked why not the dad. A legitimate question, I thought at the time. How did he ensure his kids ended up in the factory daily? And what good was it to impose a fine or prison on someone who already had no money? Who would benefit from this manufactured drama? Those were the silver bullet questions that would remain unanswered forever. Some papers went with this story. Sensationalised misery increased sales.

"Mikhail, please adjust your language," I reminded Hoodie Boy, "and start responding to my marking."

Hoodie Boy manspread in his chair, licking his lips. Intimidatingly, he looked at Sophia, who kept her eyes glued to her work and pretended he was not there. Boys' dreams were mothers' nightmares.

"This is boring. Nobody cares about Vietnam. It's far away."

"Mikhail, this is your second warning."

I wrote his name on the board and continued to teach.

"I don't care. Boring. This sucks. The Americans are losers."

"Mikhail, please be quiet,"

I added another tick next to Mikhail's name and continued teaching. Mikhail continued his programme of disruption and shouting. He earned himself an email to the overlord on duty. His presence in the academy added nothing to the class but destroyed it, academically and physically.

A few minutes after I had sent the email, a high-vis walkie-talkie-carrying, middle-aged blonde overlord arrived. Mrs Winter to the rescue. She was the Assistant Headteacher for Aspiration and Personal Development. What a nonsensical title this was. It was another one of those fake positions that sprang up all over the island. What did this lady do all day, and how was it worth 60 grand per year? This English teacher now somehow found herself in a position of having to deal with Hoodie Boy. Since overlords rarely taught lessons, they had plenty of time to be on duty, as it was called. They wandered around the factory floor elegantly but with purpose to any room where a serf could not engage kids in their lessons and where a kid had accumulated three strikes.

"Good morning," I uttered with a fake smile.

Yoga-loving vegan Mrs Winter replied with a fake smile, "Good morning, Miss, what is the matter?"

"Mikhail has difficulties following instructions. He must be removed from this lesson so everyone else can continue their exam preparations."

"Mikhail, will you please follow me?"

Hoodie Boy was not impressed by her pleas to follow him. He did not move. Instead, he grinned.

"This lesson sucks." He insisted.

Mrs Winter decided to have a short talk with Mikhail. She had to walk to him. She whispered in his ear, and his body language remained unchanged. Then she turned to me and announced, "Mikhail has assured me that he will now focus on exam preparation. There is no need for him to be removed at this time."

What wishful or deluded thinking was this? The evil of inaction facilitated the evil of action. I knew calling the overlord on duty again was a pointless exercise. Gaslighting was one of the skills they had mastered to perfection. So I continued my lesson, ignoring Hoodie Boy and the behaviour policy. I had done my job but was ignored when asked for support. Nothing new. Hoodie Boy's book was marked, and the lesson was well prepared, resourced and in line with what should be included. Yet he chose not to care. I wondered where this policeman from yesterday afternoon was.

Incompetence married to indifference, which summed up Mrs Winter. The shine of her high-vis could not compensate for how utterly useless she was. An educational leadership car crash. Apparently, the factory had imagined she was worth a lot of money when they created this position around aspiration and personal development for her nearly two years ago. Mrs Winter's job puzzled me. When the position was published, I had read the advertisement and person specification, not because I wanted to apply but because I wanted to be amused.

Someone had once written a book on bullshit jobs, and this one should be included. Everyone within the factory knew that this was an artificially created position to keep certain people in the building. Often, their role was without much impact. They had odd titles and even odder job descriptions, which needed to include as little talent as possible and could not be very specific. The application process was fake, too. It did not take a profiler to determine who would be offered the job. It was clear from the outset. An external candidate has yet to get those jobs. Within the factory, there were line managers who ran around encouraging other serfs to apply, well knowing that the position had already been given to the person it had been created for in the first place. But this whole charade had to be kept up. Some job adverts were more a formality than an opportunity for qualified people to find a job. The advertisement for Mrs Winter's position was such a formality. The show had to go on. Everything had to look prim and proper, so nobody could make any claims that jobs were handed out according to whether a face fit or not. This was an elite members' club. Admission was by invitation only.

When this teenage whisperer with zero authority walked out, I smiled at her in a faux-neutral manner.

"Thank you," I added for nothing in my head.

Hoodie smiled an evil smile at me. I smiled back at him, imagining I would meet him again ten years later when I finally worked in a prison. He would be back in my class, but this time, he would behave and not disrupt the other offenders.

The sun tickled my skin. I was surrounded by kids playing football, eating crisps and screaming. I had to push my dress down whilst balancing my scratched phone and stained cup as the wind blew despite the lovely sunshine and mild temperatures. It was break time, and the noise was unbearable. I was on the way to the staffroom, which was located in the main building. My factory still had a staffroom, but it had not yet turned into a coffee shop like in some academies, where serfs had no space to prepare lessons in peace and had to pay for their coffees. Finding an empty room was a highly unlikely undertaking, especially in the inner cities, in overcrowded factories designed decades ago for much smaller cohorts of kids.

In the staffroom, I was greeted by Ajinder, whose name meant victorious and victorious she was. When we met a few years ago, Ajinder was a teaching assistant working with little, wheelchair-bound Rachel, who needed one-to-one support in all lessons. Ajinder was not only victorious but also patient. After an abusive, forced marriage and a difficult divorce, she had fallen on her feet and completed her lifelong dream of becoming a serf. She had also found a lovely husband.

"Do you and Bella want to come over tonight?" she asked, signalling for me to sit beside her.

"Sorry, today is not good. I have to run a CPD session after school. How about Friday evening, are you free?"

"Friday it is. I will cook for us."

I could not wait. I loved going to Ajinder's as she was a talented chef who always cooked plenty of food. I usually walked out with boxes of leftovers. Bella loved hanging out with Ajinder's two kids, who were already 10 and 15, but looked after her as if she was their little sister.

Ajinder did not stop smiling, and I became suspicious.

"What's up, Jinni?"

She burst out laughing.

"Tell me about the Sunjit incident! Shame we cannot send him to Pentonville with his brother for this, innit?"

"I wish, Jinni. Did Agata tell you what

happened?" I shook my head, laughing.

"Of course, the whole factory knows."

There were only four minutes left of break time. I had to head back to my cage. Finally, I had peace and silence in my room. This was my planning lesson. I double-checked all those books from the last lesson. As foreseen, Hoodie Boy and his underlings had yet to do what they were meant to do. His book, along with the other two, had to disappear for a little bit. I put the evidence of my teaching incompetence in my bag. Like a criminal, I walked past Flora in reception with the forbidden goodies on my shoulder.

I opened the boot and put the bag in, remembering that the MOT was due soon. I had to call Justin. How cars worked and what needed doing was something I needed to learn. If the MOT people had announced that I had to spend £2000 to make my car roadworthy, I would have nodded and paid. Every year, Justin saved me from becoming an easy victim of an MOT rip-off. Sometimes, around MOT time, I thought about Ridwan, a former student who wanted to be a mechanic. I had to chase him after school to get him to complete his Jack the Ripper coursework. At the time, he made a valid point telling me he was already working in his uncle's garage. One day, he would take over the business, and Jack the Ripper would not help him in his career. A fair point, I thought. Time to find him. Ridwan, not Jack the Ripper. He would probably give me a discount. Until then, Justin would have to help.

In the car park, I got the impression that many exercise books walked out of the building into mobile hiding places to be kidnapped until the overlords were done micromanaging and justifying their fake positions with unnecessary tasks. It was not just me who had become a master in deception to remain on the payroll. Good. As a union member, I believed strongly in collective action to dislodge the elite and create better conditions for us serfs. This was another excellent example of it, albeit a secretive one. All those serfs taking books to cars had outfoxed the overlords.

TUESDAY, 12 PM

Back in my classroom, I started preparing differentiated resources for the little year 8s. I needed each worksheet in English and Polish. I checked the PowerPoint for the afternoon lessons. As soon as the bell went, I locked my room and quickly walked over to the canteen, another outbuilding. The weekly lunch duty added a bit of pocket money to my pay and meant a free lunch and 40 minutes of extra work. Every week, some kids would arrive before me. They were usually year 10s and 11s. The older A-level kids were allowed to leave the factory for lunch. The younger ones envied them. Sometimes, the A-level kids were given little shopping lists and money. They acted as middlemen for those younger kids who had the confidence to approach older ones and did not enjoy school lunches.

I ensured the queue was somewhat straight and the noise levels not as high as if Lady Gaga had just appeared on stage greeted by her adoring fans.

"Miss, please let me jump the queue," a teenage girl with long black curls shouted.

"No," I said sharply to Chantelle with a smile.

She first appeared in one of my lessons last November, having been kicked out of another local factory and placed in my Year 11 GCSE group. The overlords had warned me about this girl with a metre-long record of poor behaviour and temporary exclusions. However, I found Chantelle to be a bright girl, outspoken, yes, but also witty and interested and able in history. She was a leader who got herself in trouble because she was not afraid to speak up or, better, shout out, like the one time when she was pretty new to the factory and dangled a pack of tampons in the young PE teacher's face, informing him that she was on her period and would not take part in PE. He could do very little about it. The way he looked around indicated that all he wanted to do was for the floor to open and for him to disappear underground. Instead, Chantelle's voice level drew a reasonably sizable crowd of horrified and bemused kids. The boys especially were grossed out. The girls did not know whether to smile or walk away. It was a scene from a movie. Away from the playground and in my lessons, Chantelle had shown herself to be a hard worker who would probably go far in life.

At the end of my duty, I jumped the queue

myself. Teacher's privilege.

"Double apple crumble without custard, for you Miss?" Laura, Carlos's wife who worked at the factory as a dinner lady, asked.

"You know me well. Pedro has grown so much. I spoke to Carlos last night; he has shown me the latest videos. Any idea when you are flying to Brazil next?"

Laura's eyes sparkled.

"If all goes well, at the end of July," she added, "might not come back."

I looked forward to a few minutes of peace with my spaghetti bolognese and the best school dessert. After repeatedly asking kids to tidy up after themselves and avoiding two food fights, eating surrounded by kids did not seem appealing. I chose the safety of the staffroom. A big mistake, as I would shortly find out.

I walked behind two Year 11 boys. In the oversized plimsolls, the boy on the left stumbled and nearly fell. His friend thought it was hilarious. The stumble boy had probably arrived at the factory in the incorrect shoes. He had to be punished by wearing factory plimsolls for the rest of the day. It looked as though he would be punished by breaking his neck and falling over himself. Would the factory have to pay for this? Was there a fall in plimsolls insurance? A few serfs sat down over tin soups, and three were waiting their turn at the microwave. There were never any overlords in the staffroom. They went to the secure area, and some were out and about on duty. Food was compared, kids discussed, and the blow job request had already travelled the entire factory. Some serfs commented on Sunjit's lack of engagement in lesson material, his family in general, and his convict brother, an ex-student.

"I think the overlords have gone mad," Ajinder said.

"Why?"

"Yesterday evening in the year team meeting, Malik suggested that we call the kids who oversleep in the mornings to ensure they would turn up on time."

"I don't think so. It's called parenting.``

"Exactly. I can hardly get my kids out of bed. And as soon as they are up, we have breakfast together," Ajinder explained, "the factory can't expect us to sacrifice our families even more. Right?"

"I refuse to act like a parent. We have our families, and this is a job. Never forget it, Jinni," I continued, "if we fell over dead this afternoon, they would replace us by tomorrow morning and complain about the inconvenience."

"Exactly, Malik has all the time in the world because his missus gave up her teaching career so he could have one. They are probably creating a fake position for him as we speak."

"His face fits right into the factory ethos. He is great at charming the overlords."

"Say it louder!" Ajinder agreed.

"You know he is in the union?"

"What? Stop it." Ajinder did not believe me.

"Yes, but he would never be seen at a union meeting or, even worse, a strike. He knows that any association with the workshy serfs who demand fairer treatment, better pay and improved working conditions would be used against any future applications for overlord positions."

“Speaking of the devil,” Ajinder said when the staffroom door opened.

Mr Malik. the Head of Year 9, a tall, mid-30s Business Teacher, shouted towards me.

"Hey Eva, you have a visitor."

I was puzzled.

"A visitor? Who is it?"

Mr Malik smiled. He was amused.

"It's blow job Sunjit's daddy."

"Now?" I replied, slightly annoyed.

"Yes, come on, let's go."

"Jinni, protect my food, please."

Ajinder nodded. I followed Mr Malik, who lived in the factory from at least seven in the morning until seven at night. We walked with Flora, who opened the gate to the forbidden kingdom, the promised land. She let us both into the area that could only be accessed by the overlords. Sunjit's father had arrived at the factory because the factory, specifically Mr Malik, had called him for a meeting. I wondered how Sunjit's dad could make it here so quickly, in the middle of the day. Did he have a hobby job, too?

Although I appreciated that Mr Malik was doing something about the blow job incident, I wished he had asked me about a meeting time that would have worked better for me. Lunchtime was no such time. This is yet another sign that Mr Malik's union membership was as fake as his future position as Assistant Headteacher for something or other. As a union member, he should have known that meetings during lunch should only be arranged if everyone agreed. I wished I had stayed in the canteen and eaten there.

Flora guided us to a small meeting room. These nice areas with posh coffee from fancy machines and expensive biscuits were reserved for the overlords and their visitors, like politicians and, on occasion, the press, but also the parents of the worst offenders. The serfs bought their kettles. They hid them under their desks in their rooms, hoping no overlord would ever notice.

I opened the door to the meeting room, and there was Sunjit's father, an exact copy of his overweight son but 35 years his senior and a few more kilos. He sat on one of the fancy chairs; better, he was stuck in one of those, already in tears. He was ashamed, apologising repeatedly as soon as he saw me. I could not help but feel sorry for him, but I was also hungry and wanted this over quickly. I needed the help of Samira, another teaching assistant who could translate. Together with Mr Malik, I tried to calm down Sunjit's father. I accepted the apology he had offered. Like I had done many times before. Teachers were charity shops for forgiveness. The parents would apologise for the behaviour of their little darlings. Factories would label such incidents as one-off incidents. Nothing would ever change.

Those incidents were nothing new, nothing to lose thought over. Had my lesson been more interesting and tailored towards Sunjit's prior knowledge and interests, this question surely would not have come up. Really, in the eyes of the overlords, whose kingdom I had been allowed to enter, I had to rethink my teaching strategies. I was to blame. It was my fault that a 14-year-old boy had deliberately asked an inappropriate question. The fingers were clearly pointing in my direction. The direction of incompetence. As punishment, I had to waste my time on a meeting with the father, which would make no difference to anyone. Sunjit would continue to behave the way he behaved. In addition, I had to complete an incident report form. All extra work, freebie work. Unpaid. No time allowance was made for these things that happened every day. I returned quickly to the staffroom, where I had less than five minutes to eat lunch.

TUESDAY, 1:50 PM

Walking over to the languages department for my Urdu cover lesson, I thought I must not forget to thank Agata for having already referred the blow job distraction to Mr Malik. Agata was amazing as a teaching assistant and a person. We got on extremely well. Sometimes, she came to my place for dinner and a few drinks. Agata could hold her drinks very well, much better than I could, and she had a big voice and an even bigger laugh. Her platinum blonde short bob with dark roots made her stand out at the factory. With a master's in education, she was entirely overqualified for her current and previous work at Pizza Express. Most nights, she would take the train to London to teach adults her native language. Agata saved all her money for travelling. Each holiday she found some bargain and travelled the world. On her return, she would tell of elephants in Thailand and dancing in Cuba. Bella hung on to Agata's every word. Teaching assistants and friends like Agatha were irreplaceable. Of course, everyone was replaceable in the eyes of the overlords and inspectors.

The twenty Urdu words I had picked up when I was with Bella's dad had to suffice in impressing the kids and making them believe that I knew what I was doing and what they were saying. In room 20, it was showtime.

"As-salaam-alaikum. Aap kaise hou?"

Silence.

I felt like Roman general Maximus Decimus Meridius in the movie Gladiator, who had asked the crowd in the Colosseum whether they were entertained. My Urdu greeting, combined with a poker face, had silenced the group. All of them were native speakers. I walked around the class handing out the worksheets that had been printed by the head of the department but sent in by the regular serf just before 7 am this morning. Factories demanded cover work. Thus, around the country, serfs with coughs and temperatures created work for kids who would ignore said work because a cover teacher taught the lesson. In the eyes of the kids, this did not count as a real lesson.

"Guys, this is how this lesson will go," I said, "we ignore each other. You do your work, I do mine, and we will be fine. Any questions?"

The group nodded. For the rest of the lesson,

the kids were busy with their worksheets, chatting quietly with each other, which I did not mind. I logged onto the computer in the corner of the room and checked my emails. Blow job, boy Sunjit had already written an apology. It was insincere. He would have been made to do it under the shouting and keen eye of Mr Malik. He would probably spend the rest of the day in internal exclusion doing nothing, creating more vacuum in his brain. I had to pretend to care, but I did not. I ignored the email. I also ignored the email for volunteers to take the kids to Thorpe Park on a Saturday. And I ignored the email that asked serfs to sign up for the annual summer fair again on a Saturday. Over the years, I had learnt that no email was important. If I ignored the first email, most people did not bother emailing a second time. This strategy meant that I had fewer problems to deal with. The bell went, and as nobody got hassled during the Urdu lesson, everyone left happy, on time, and on good terms.

"Khuda hafiz and goodbye."

Outside the classroom, a tall, fitness-obsessed man in a suit was already waiting for me and the class to leave. He could easily have been an insurance broker but was, in fact, Mr Josiah, who also had to cover a language lesson just like me. He pushed right past me before I got out of the room.

"Miss, why have you removed yourself from the WhatsApp group I set up two weeks ago?" He asked in disbelief.

Although he looked and behaved like a member of the PE department, he was my head of department, the head of Humanities. Just like me, he usually taught history and politics.

"It's all about sharing resources and exchanging ideas. We all want the kids to do well. Don't you want to be part of a team, a family?"

Everything he did was done enthusiastically, so I wondered what he was taking or when he would collapse. He followed me into the corridor and waited for my answer. When most of the kids had disappeared into their classrooms, I replied.

"Frankly, no. I don't want to be part of a family. I have a family at home. I don't need to be adopted. I am here for work," I added for the money internally.

Having grown up under communism, I had no more interest in being part of a team or a group. I was teamed out, not interested in community events, family feelings at work or weekend team-building exercises. All I wanted to do was go to work, do my job well and be left alone. In my opinion, team events were just forced on people. In reality, every grown-up should just work with whoever else happens to walk around their workplace. If people needed to go to events to learn how to work with each other first, maybe, just maybe, they were not ready to be employed. I got on with most people, even those I did not like, and they would not have noticed it.

A WhatsApp group was highly intrusive and did not make anyone's life easier. There were already emails, briefings, meetings, shared online spaces, resources uploaded in different forums and now WhatsApp groups. Nothing was cutting-edge about this. It was too much. Factories did not collapse 30 years previously when this technology did not exist.

"But, Miss, you might benefit from it. Someone might share something that you can use in your lessons."

He was one of those highly motivated serfs competing with Mr Malik for the attention of the overlords. He was also searching for the next best fake position created. He needed to be noticed by one of the overlords, who would then push him forward. Mr Josiah constantly walked around with a green or dark red shake in one of those containers influencers carried on Instagram. Although he was married with three kids, he flirted extensively with any female under thirty, and he had rightly earned himself a Casanova reputation in the factory. I had little time for this guy who boasted about his 5:2 fasting diet. I saw him for what he was. A noisy boss who brown-nosed his way into a higher salary bracket. A man who had little respect for his wife and family. He is a waste of space, a sad leftover from the 1950s who was using innovation not to make the world a better palace but to further his agenda.

"If the school would like me to join a WhatsApp group, the school should provide me with a phone and pay the bill. In the meantime, you can email me Sir. See you later."

I heard his chin hit the floor. WhatsApp groups were everywhere: at work, in friendship groups, and at Bella's primary factory. I could not comprehend why anyone would want to be in a group with 25 to 50 parents, for example, some of them Über-parents. Forgotten PE kits, misplaced items of clothing, yet another birthday party, and cake sales to fund whatever the government should be paying for. All this was in Bella's class WhatsApp group for parents. If anyone dared to take themselves out of those groups, like I had at work, that would be considered social suicide. A crime that was punishable by public shaming. A clear sign of child neglect. In reality, most parents would not have spoken to each other if they had not had kids in the same class. I had not taken myself out of this parent group because I did not want Bella to be looked at as if she was neglected by her full-time working, antisocial single mum. There were probably already separate mother groups discussing me and others like me.

The A-level historians waited outside my room and moaned that they had to stand in the sun for a few minutes. They were focused and wanted the exams to happen now unless Rahman, the pack's leader, decided that today was not his day.

"Miss, why don't we get study leave?"

"Rahman, I don't make the rules. Please take your AirPods out now."

"Miss, they are my hearing aids."

The class laughed, and even I had to smile. This young man was not feeling the vibes to do any work. Not only did Rahman refuse to take out his AirPods, but he also threatened everyone in the classroom with peeing in a plastic bottle right here in front of us. I was alarmed when he started to walk around fumbling with his trousers, the bottle at hand. He quickly collected his three strikes, triggering the arrival of an overlord.

On duty this lesson was Mr Sullivan. A scary ex-army type of guy who intimidated serfs and kids alike. He walked with a limp but refused to use a cane, probably to stop himself from using it on the kids or serfs he considered a waste of space. Mr Sullivan was the overlord in charge of pupil behaviour and attitudes, and he was well placed because he had all the makings of a dictator. Unlike the useless overlord from the Hoodie Boy lesson, Mr Sullivan appeared quickly and as soon as the door opened, the class fell silent; such was his effect on everyone.

"Miss, what happened?" Mr Sullivan asked without any emotion on his face.

His keys on a black leather lanyard swang by the side of his limping leg like a signature move. He looked like a jailor.

"Rahman is attempting to pee in a plastic bottle in class," I replied equally emotionlessly.

One psychopath against another.

"Get out, boy." Mr Sullivan thundered.

Rahman did not dare to refuse. Everyone had stopped breathing, and nobody had eye contact with anyone else. Most kids stared at their books until the door slammed shut. Kids looked around, wondering whether they were allowed to breathe again. Mr Sullivan could easily have been a character in a US Army movie with his ginger buzz-cut hair and intimidating stature. His modus operandi was to be as scary as possible. With Rahman having disappeared to an unknown location, I could continue the revision lesson on Thatcher's social housing sell-off and the deregulation of the City of London. The bell went.

"Please sit down, Jennifer," I said, "I have not finished."

"But Miss, the bell went."

"I am the bell."

Jennifer sat back down again, her face annoyed.

"Have a look at the resources I uploaded online. There are some funky videos which you will find useful when revising. Now, you are dismissed."

I loved that some teachers took the time to create little revision videos. They were short and snappy and explained quickly what must be done in exam questions. Teachers who managed to create this type of content online were superteachers. They helped countless kids before exams and teachers because they could easily refer to them.

TUESDAY, 4 PM

I was asked to run a professional development session on questioning this afternoon. Ideally, they were tailored to what the serfs needed to improve or the skills they wanted to expand, but in reality, people just signed up for anything on offer and did not seem too repetitive. The overlords considered me an outstanding teacher, which sounded nice but got me to do even more work. Other serfs would come to observe me. I had to coach and mentor early careers and experienced serfs. Being outstanding was a trap, and I had decided to manipulate my future observations only to get the grade "good". I would make a low-priority effort. This way, the overlords would ask me for less of this unpaid work, but I would keep my job.

Nearly 25 serfs mingled in the hall. They had signed up for my session. A few would have Improving Questioning as one of their three performance management targets. Some were here hoping this would be a bearable session without stupid tasks. Others probably hoped this would be one of the sessions that would finish on time because they knew I had to pick up Bella.

Usually, at this time, at least one overlord was in attendance at each session across the school. They were snooping under the disguise of wanting to partake. The overlord on double agent duty was Mrs Winter, the same Mrs Winter who, earlier in the day, had been incapable of saving my lesson from being destroyed by Hoodie Boy.

I turned my slideshow on quickly, took the register and gave my whistle-stop tour on questioning. My colleagues took the kids' role, but I was still the entertainer. The session went by without any significant incidents. Everyone was on top behaviour. We all had the same aim. Get out of here as quickly as possible. Mrs Winter nodded approvingly from the corner. The serfs thought up open-ended questions for their lessons. I completed the session on time, grabbed my marking bag and walked right out of the hall past the overlords' playground.

Sometimes, continued professional development sessions took place outside the factory, and I had been to a few. As terrorists now lurked around every corner, it was no surprise that I had to attend a training session on spotting the radical kid last year. This was in addition to spotting which girl was in danger of female genital mutilation and which child needed support because they were carers looking after other family members. Everything that was not done by the rest of society, parents or the community had to be done by serfs, who were also expected to teach outstanding lessons at all times and to sacrifice their families, relationships and sanity at the altar of a failing education system created by politicians who had never attended the state factory system.

A teacher was no longer what the dictionary said they were: someone who teaches in a factory. No, these days, a serf had to have several personalities; no wonder there were so many teachers with mental health problems ready to leave the profession. A serf must be a social worker, counsellor, psychiatrist, police officer, parent, travel agent, librarian, negotiator, detective, clown, comedian, or actor. Those roles had to be carried out simultaneously, but the pay did not reflect that. Mostly, I contemplated, serfs had to be actors. Our whole day was one big theatre session with an unwilling audience and extra harsh critics.

TUESDAY, 5 PM

I drove off the premises with my hidden books in the boot and new books to mark. I passed the local football stadium I had recently been to with Rumi. Her company had given her free tickets. It was an interesting psychological study into conformity and aggression. I had gone undercover and sat with the supporters of the team I did not support, or better, the team Rumi did not support, because I never really took interest in football, maybe in the players but not in the game. However, those tickets were free. It did not matter who played and how well they did. Sitting in the wrong area gave me a bit of a kick, like I was a spy or something. I had to be on high alert, not drifting off. My fake team might have scored any second. I had to act like a real fan, like I cared. Jumping up, clapping and screaming, all of it. The complete fan programme had to be acted out. I had to be in character.

I needed to get angry at the opponent, Rumi's team. Had I failed to do so, suspicion would have arisen, and eyes would have been on us rather than the ball. This was hard work. But it was fun, too. The characters at a football game were interesting. Some spectators believed they were the actual managers. Others were just philosophers. I preferred the latter. At least they were not going to bash anyone's head in. They just imagined they knew a lot and would explain their grasp of the subject using a pleasant voice. The former, oh dear, what scary creatures. They would attack anyone appearing to do their team any injustice. Theirs was a total physical effort. Every muscle in their face and body was alert. They were ready to tell everyone who did not want to know that the referee had made grave mistakes. They would shout at the flag person running along the field, the coach, the players, the owner of the club, the sponsors, the masseuse, and god knows who else. It had been an exciting evening out, but I did not need a repeat. Rumi's team won.

Traffic was slow. I just wanted to get to Bella and make it home to start cooking. Bella, too, seemed tired. She was not talkative in the car and had difficulty opening her eyes. I watched her in the back mirror, letting her relax rather than chat. Three minutes before we arrived at home, Bella fell asleep. I carried another set of exercise books inside, pushed the recycling bin back into its place and then carried Bella into the flat. I put her on the sofa so as not to wake her.

Tonight, I felt like sausages, mash and sauerkraut. Bella would like that dinner, too. Both of us loved mash. The more salt there was in it, the better. I turned on my laptop and found a short real-life murder documentary on YouTube, which I watched with one eye while cooking. As soon as the show started, I knew who had done it. It was always the same pattern. A girl met a boy; both were very young. They got together, sometimes married, and had a kid shortly after and then domestic violence would start. The woman, realising she was with a waste man, wanted to leave. He decided the only way out for her was death, as if the woman was property. Awful. Those men, why could they not just let the women go? Often, those crimes were labelled crimes of passion. I thought of them as crimes of calculation. There was no residue of morality left in men who committed such crimes.

The mash was done, sausages and the sauerkraut were on the table. I got the mustard and the plates out when Bella woke up just in time like a puppy, having heard a crisp bag being opened. I quickly shut the laptop.

"Hey, Bella, let's eat. Go wash your hands, please, and we can start."

"OK, Mami. I can smell sausages and mash." Bella smiled sleepily.

"Bella, tell me, what was the best part of your day?"

Bella looked up at the ceiling as if the answer was written there.

"Hm, the best part of my day was when we learned about the Romans."

"Did you already learn that the Romans made it all the way to England and that we even have Roman roads here in town?"

"Really, and the Romans walked on those roads?"

"Yes, they walked on those roads a long, long time ago."

"Wow."

"What do you think, shall we go to Rome in the summer?"

Bella, chewing her sausage, nodded.

"Ok, let's try and do this, but first, you are going to Austria with your grandparents; how excited are you about this?"

"Very excited. I will go on a plane, and we will go skiing in Austria and have Kaiserschmarrn."

I was envious of the food they would eat.

TUESDAY, 7:30 PM

After dinner, Bella sat with her numeracy homework. She did not look happy. Numeracy was not her strong point, but today, she struggled more than usual.

"Mami, can you help me please? I don't understand this."

"Let's see what Mami, the maths wizard, can do."

Bella smiled. As a teacher and someone with an A-level in maths, I indeed should have been able to handle this primary maths, but shock and horror, I was not. Why did they explain everything in such a complicated manner? And what was this task even asking? I was perplexed. Also, why were there no textbooks to use like in other countries where even little kids had books that explained everything for each subject for their age group? What was it with all those separate copies, and why were exercise books not taken home daily? After ten minutes of trying to figure out how to do this task, I noticed how I was about to lose patience with myself. Bella was by now just quiet and sad.

"Bella, listen, I will write an email to your teacher telling her that we tried this homework together, but we could not do it, ok? Don't worry, I am sure Miss will explain this to you again tomorrow."

"Ok." Bella agreed.

My B in A-level maths was no match for this primary numeracy task. I sat down to email the teacher whilst Bella had a shower. An answer would never materialise. I understood why. I knew. We serfs knew. We were all caught in the same matrix entangled in teacher standards, OFSTED criteria, so-called deep dives into data and documentation and relentless supervision from the overlords. I often contemplated why textbooks were so frowned upon in most factories. I used to like getting new books at the end of my eight summer holidays during the last week of August. Back home, we had a book for every subject. When we were ill or our parents helped with homework, a rare occurrence, they could just use the book to explain things. The single sheet, stuck in exercise books nonsense, was frustrating for me. I felt helpless. A system designed for failure.

This night's marking was a bit easier because the little year 7s still tried to make everything look pretty. Their answers were shorter than the older kids' responses. When Bella came out of the shower, she demanded a piggy bag into bed. I obliged and walked into her bedroom with a happy Bella on my back.

"Which story are we reading tonight? And who is reading?"

Bella ran to her bookshelf and got a book called The Worst Witch. I smiled and had to think of my factory's CEO. I wondered whether Mrs Viper was the main character in this story.

"I read. Ok, Mami?"

"Sounds great."

Around 9.30 pm, I woke up in Bella's bed. She was fast asleep next to me. The witch book on her belly. I wanted to stay and sleep, but only some of the exercise books on the kitchen table had been marked. I tucked her in, took the book, kissed her and quietly shut the door. Just before eleven, all was done. I was allowed to sleep, too.

WEDNESDAY, 8:10 AM

PE Joshua jumped right at me on my way into the staffroom. This is why I could not be part of the PE team; they were already zooming around like locomotives before the average person had had their morning coffee.

"Have you read my email about sports day," he asked passionately, "we need to get teams together. Do you think you will run the relay this year?"

"Not yet," I smiled, "What on earth are you thinking? Me in a relay? You cannot pay me enough to see me participate in any sports day activity."

"Come on, Eva, you can do it. Let me know when you change your mind."

"That would be never," I replied, looking through the paperwork in my pigeonhole opposite the staffroom door.

"Why Eva? You strike me as a sporty person."

On the other side of the staffroom, I heard

the chatter of the serfs who ate their breakfast porridge at the factory. Something I had never understood.

"I am a sporty person, but not in public," I said, "I have always disliked sports day. In my backyard, we used to bunk sports day and meet our friends instead."

"No way, Eva, you are lying." PE Joshua was surprised.

"Nobody followed up because there were no detentions," I smiled, "Sorry to be a disappointment. I am sure Cunningham and the other overlords will join in."

On my way out, I threw the invitation for the Friday staff social into the recycling bin. I was anti-social. Not in an ASBO kind of way. I did not cause trouble. My antisocial was the *quiet, leave me alone* kind of antisocial. PE staff ranked high on the sociability scale. They were social butterflies, mixing and mingling without inhibitions. Their extroverted nature made others feel drawn to them. They enjoyed the centre stage.

A moment of sunshine entered my morning in the form of Carlos, who waved from the opposite side of the corridor with his huge smile. I waved back to this long-term inmate but had no time to talk. I continued to walk over to my room. In the distance, I saw a witch-like figure hovering outside my classroom. It was Mrs

Fry, the Assistant Headteacher for Stakeholder Engagement. Who were these stakeholders, and what was Mrs Fry doing to engage them? At least she was not the Assistant Headteacher for Shareholder Engagement. Stakeholder Engagement and CEO were terms stolen directly from the corporate rule book, I thought. No wonder kids had become data sets, and serfs were easily replaceable. We lived in a corporate education nightmare.

I felt my stomach turning into knots. These people did not come to a serf's classroom unless one's performance or form group's performance was deemed unacceptable. Mrs Fry could easily have been a guard in Zimbardo's Stanford Prison Experiment. The way she held herself was scary. She had long entered the retirement age category and walked like a robot. She was probably used as a blueprint for AI robots. The very robots which one day would kill humanity, according to my predictions. But by then, I would either be dead or living in my little house in Sicily. Those robots would not cross the water to get there. Mrs Fry had not retired because she was a control freak, or maybe her family did not want her at home. This would be understandable. Apart from my first year, I usually had little to do with her. This corrections officer was also responsible for professional tutoring and looked after the newbies, including myself.

"Good morning," she greeted me with a stern face under her short, grey hair.

The robot lady did not show any emotion, which was emotion enough.

"I have to speak to you."

Of course, she had to. Why else would she leave the sanctuary that was her one-person office with a tax-funded coffee machine? I fumbled with my keys and opened the door to my classroom.

"Good morning. Come in, please," I uttered, putting my heavy bags on a desk closest to the door. I was angry with myself for getting nervous around those overlords.

"I will come straight to the point. Your form group behaved disgustingly in Mr Ajim's ICT lesson yesterday afternoon," the robot continued businesslike, "I am very disappointed in your form group."

I was shocked. Cold sweat formed on my neck.

"I am sorry. What happened?" I asked timidly.

"Joshua and Imran disturbed the class by accessing pornographic materials on the school's computers just when the CEO conducted a learning walk in the ICT department. This was unacceptable; you must deal with those students and your form. Your group was a disgrace, and you must change this. "

And that was it. The robot witch walked off towards the main building. I almost expected her to turn around, whizz a magic wand and send me off into banishment; such was the atmosphere created by her.

I stood there perplexed and angry, but at the same time, I also felt amused. A washing machine of feelings. *Your group, your responsibility, ICT lesson, porn, learning walk* my head was spinning. I had only been at the factory for 15 minutes. I could not figure out how any of this was my fault. And although I had taken on the job of human reproduction, I had not given birth to any of those little people involved. None of those kids had left my body. Yet, here I was, getting a telling-off from someone who taught three lessons of top-set English per week and spent the rest of her day causing headaches for others.

Most serfs were given a form group. This was not a choice we freely made. It was a task slapped on like many others. It came with teaching, no matter what subject someone chose. My form was a lovely bunch. They were kind, friendly and chatty. They treated each other well. They were not rowdy. They won most of the form competitions even though they never tried. Joshua had never caused any trouble. Yes, he was late sometimes, but he was never in trouble with the overlords. Imran had driven his dad's car into a wall at 14 but was not a Hoodie Boy who regularly caused trouble. Neither came equipped with the mindset to destroy something or someone. I had been teaching a separate lesson when two students from my form group concluded that porn on a school computer would add value to the ICT lesson. I had no control over this, and yet I was blamed. How ridiculous. This made me angry. I also had no control over the IT system and what could and could not be accessed. This day was already a mess before it had even begun. But I could not stand around contemplating how to deal with this situation. I had to set up my first lesson, turn the computer and whiteboard on, get books out and get to the morning briefing on time.

WEDNESDAY, 8:25 AM

Confused and feeling like I was entering detention, I slowly walked back to the main building to be on time for the staff briefing. Along the way, I ignored staff and kids residing in my little world, thinking about what to do about this porn situation.

The staff room was brimming; everyone had squeezed in. The daily morning briefings in the factory were of utmost importance. One could not be late or absent unless one were on morning duty or attending one's funeral.

General chatting in the staff room became silent, and a pin drop could be heard. There they were, floating in on an invisible red carpet rolled out for them. The overlords had left their sanctuary behind to enter the real world. The show was about to begin. The Director for Finance, Mrs Brad, opened and held open the door. Next was her sister-in-law, Assistant Headteacher for School Improvement,

Mrs Jackson, followed by Assistant Headteacher for Stakeholder Engagement, Mrs Fry, aka Robot Witch, who had just fried me. Tensions rose, and there she was. A swan under the protection of the crown bathing in the sun, the CEO, Mrs Viper, entered the stage, followed by her closest allies Mr Sullivan, the Assistant Headteacher for Pupil Behaviour and Attitude, Mrs Winter, the Assistant Headteacher for Aspiration and Personal Development and babyfaced Mr Cunningham, Assistant Headteacher for Curriculum and Assessment, closely followed by his buddy Mr Walsh, Assistant Headteacher for Teaching and Learning and last but not least the Deputy Chief Executive Mr Adamsky. Here was the creme de la creme of leadership in factories. The people who taught little but talked lots. The ones that went to meetings to prepare for more meetings. The micromanagers of the factories. The ones who, from time to time, joined OFSTED on their excursions to other schools to drag down the work done there by other serfs. To point fingers at failures. This charade was worth more than half a million pounds and could be found in a similar form in most state secondaries nationwide. What a spectacle these entrance shows were.

The staffroom door was shut, and the overlords positioned themselves, almost like the politburo in pre-1990 Eastern Europe. Mrs Viper, the CEO, took to the centre surrounded by an entourage of willing servants. With dramatic effect, she waited, scanning every face, taking an internal register of absentees, before addressing everyone.

"Good morning, colleagues."

Colleagues? I wondered what a sick joke this was. Wasn't a colleague a person with whom one worked in a profession or business, like a coworker type of person? As if those people in the front worked with any of the serfs. More cynical sarcasm.

This 63-year-old pigeon-faced, spectacled hag without a hair out of place was worshipped by her collaborators, who exhibited uncritical acceptance. Most kids and staff feared her. I wished for the retirement age to be lowered, not for myself, but so that this woman would crawl into some hole never to return. On her way, she should take Mrs Fry along. But they did not leave because of their desire for immortality. They aimed to reach education heaven. One day, they would haunt the school grounds as ghosts, ensuring the worship continued.

After Mrs Viper had completed her little well-rehearsed speech, she gave the room to the other overlords. Now, they were allowed to contribute to factory improvement. They took turns announcing that which had already been emailed twice this week. Only then was the room given to the serfs.

No one learned anything they did not already know. No one was inspired or motivated by this morning's show. None of this helped teaching and learning. Apart from the overlord crew and those few who aspired to be overlords, nobody wanted to be in this room. The ones with fanatical devotion did not mind wasting their mornings. Everyone else had real work to do, yet here we were. This extravaganza had an alienating effect on serfs.

"Hey Eva, what's up? Show me that cute gap between your teeth." Ajinder tried to sound positive. She had noticed my hanging shoulders and expressionless face.

"My form group is in trouble. Some boys watched porn yesterday as Viper slithered in during their ICT lesson. Now I somehow need to sort this out."

Ajinder started to laugh behind her hand.

"Oh my god, this is brilliant. I wish there were a recording of Viper's face. Can you imagine? She has probably never seen anything like it."

Ajinder's laugh was infectious. In no time, I was laughing too.

"Look, you were teaching your lesson. This is your form, but they are not your kids. What were you meant to do? This was out of your hands," she encouraged me, "Don't blame yourself. If kids can access that content, the factory must fix its IT system."

Ajinder hugged me. She was the type of friend everyone needed at work. She was married at 18 after having been told her grandma was unwell in India. She found herself in her family's village with her grandma well and happy because this granny had organised Ajinder's marriage without her knowledge or consent. For two weeks, she had tried to convince her parents that her first cousin would not be a great match. The pressure from her family and her village had been overbearing. She could not return to England unless she agreed, so she did, just one month after completing her A levels. She married a man she had met once when she was 12 on a family holiday to India and then again at her wedding. Her now ex-husband, whose name she had never spoken in front of me, was three years older, and he seemed to be ok with this arrangement. In a huge ceremony through which she cried whilst everyone else danced and ate, her previous life finished, and hell on earth started. After years of miscarriages and domestic violence, at some point around her 25th birthday, she ended up in hospital, and the police got involved. Her husband fled, probably back to India, and Ajinder went to a women's shelter. There, she rebuilt her life, got a divorce and found a job and a place to live. After that, Ajinder had little contact with her family. She also had no intentions of ever returning to her village. Maybe because of this terrible experience, Ajinder had become a drop-in centre for her friends and colleagues for anyone needing counselling, life advice or cheering up. She always knew what to say.

When I returned to my classroom, my form had already lined up outside. They were quiet because they knew what was coming. They sensed my tension.

"Good morning."

Some murmured a reply. All sat down, just opening their books to complete silent reading. I sat down, too, taking the register in a low voice. Having done so, I asked Joshua and Imran to go to the front of the class to bring their chairs and sit with me. Joshua and Imran tried to have a face that was expressionless but positive. The rest of the group was thinking of ways to look as if they were reading whilst simultaneously listening to the conversation in the front of the room.

"Guys, what was this porn business in yesterday's ICT lesson all about?"

Silence.

Embarrassment.

I had asked neither quietly nor noisily, but I felt the rest of the class had stopped breathing, wishing for ears the size of satellite dishes. I saw the corner of Joshua's mouth pull upwards into a little smile. On seeing this, Imran followed. They were trying not to look at each other, but it was impossible because they did not want to look at me either.

"I am sorry," Joshua whispered, and Imran joined him. Together, they were sorry, and I was thinking how far I was meant to take this. It was not my turn to talk about porn with those boys. The parents might take offence to that. This kind of talk needed a permission slip. I wondered why Mrs Viper had not dealt with this yesterday. Had she been too busy writing education policy for her future job? I carried on asking whether they understood why it was inappropriate to look at porn in ICT lessons.

"Yes, miss." The boys answered in sync.

This was Head of Year pay scale material, not classroom serf pay scale. I did not hand out a detention or inform their parents. The Head of Year could deal with this. I decided not to address the whole class as they had probably already been shouted at by some overlord yesterday afternoon. The rest of the class had not committed any crimes. They needed no punishment.

I positioned myself next to the door, breathing

in the lovely May air, watching the uniformed kids move from one factory area to another like ants on a mission. From behind, I heard Nazma's voice. Nazma was the fashion queen among the teaching assistants, and she was extremely competent. What she lacked in size, she made up in noise. She could run the class without a serf. I had often told her to complete teacher training, but Nazma mentioned she was happy helping kids one-on-one or in smaller groups. Seeing burnt-out serfs around her did not motivate Namza to apply for teacher training. The job only appealed to her a little.

"I have already been told off by the overlords today."

"Don't take it personally," Nazma remarked supportingly, "They need to justify their pay and walk around being critical of what we do. It gives them a purpose."

"I suppose you are right. I love your headscarf. Your girls must fight over it."

"My eldest is forever stealing my scarves. Can you believe it? Nothing is safe from her. Soon, it will be the make-up as well."

"You bet."

Here came the first kid. Blonde Finlay was a bright boy who often got into trouble for asking good questions at the wrong moment. I had decided that Finlay was a fun character to have in class, cheeky but intelligent, a little entertainer.

"Is Miss your backup teacher?" he asked on his way while looking at Nazma.

"Yes," Nazma said, "I am the backup teacher."

Twenty-seven more youngsters followed, some slowly and half asleep, others full of energy drinks and sugar from the local corner shop next to the school gates.

"Why do girls have to go to school anyway?" Jibril asked out of nowhere. He seemed upset about my arrangements for the group work task.

"So that one day when they are married to a nasty man, they can leave because they will have the education and qualifications to find a job," I said, "That's why."

Silence.

The boys were stunned. The girls smiled shyly, as did Nazma, who worked by the window with a group of kids. Jibril had picked the wrong lesson for such comments. I had grown up in a society where dads had changed their kids' nappies in the 70s, had stayed at home with sick kids, and knew how to cook and clean without being reminded twenty times over. A country where women went to university and had full-time jobs whether they wanted them or not. Jibril had to put his sexism in the bin and engage in group work on the Crusades with girls in his group, whether he liked it or not.

I felt excited for my next lesson. Year 9s Citizenship on domestic violence. It is no easy feat, but necessary. The group was late. They had PE, which was the furthest away from my classroom. I had planned for the class to watch a social experiment on YouTube, but it took quite some time before the class settled into YouTube mode and was receptive to seeing something.

In the days when I was at school, there was no internet, YouTube or DVD players. If we were lucky, the teacher would wheel in a small desk or tray-like construction with an average-sized television on top and a video player. I and my classmates knew not to make any sound, not to ask what film this was and how long we would watch it for, not to comment on Josephine's hairdo or Marcus's head being in the line of sight. No, we would be dead silent because we knew one question and one wrong move by any of us would see the TV being rolled back into the cupboard, where it would remain for the rest of the academic year. Nobody wanted this. That is why we had learnt to be silent. Our teacher did not take any nonsense, shouting out or endless idiotic questions. In return, we watched a film once or twice a year.

My kids' attention spans did not allow for such a scenario. Questions over questions, requests to move seats, complaints about someone's hair, head, or elbow, requests for subtitles, pauses, and explanations of plots were standard, as were complaints about the poor quality of material, the poor editing or stupid music. Therefore, watching a clip or a film became more of a headache than teaching a normal lesson.

Eight minutes into the lesson, I was finally able to start the clip in which a woman was verbally abusing her boyfriend and also pushing him. All this happened in a little park where people enjoyed their lunch break on what must have been a hot summer's day. Most of the kids giggled, laughed and found it hilarious that a man was treated like this by a woman, but when in the clip, the scenario switched to a man shoving around his partner, they became quiet. After that, a productive discussion on domestic violence unfolded until Max, who had a different take on the issue, explained that when a husband beat his wife, it was a family problem, not a criminal matter. Such statements were not uncommon, and I had dealt with them before. Still, it made me sad that there was a young generation of boys who questioned education for girls and who believed domestic violence was somehow acceptable. And this one lesson on domestic violence would probably not change much. This fight against sexism and violence was a daily fight, in addition to teaching regular subjects. It added to the fatigue I and many others felt. It frustrated girls as well as female staff and drained our energy.

WEDNESDAY, 11:20 AM

For now, it was break time. I wanted tea without having to walk to the main building. I crouched under my desk and plugged in the kettle, which should not have been in my room in the first place, but hot water was hard to come by if one was placed in an outbuilding. Getting up, I banged my head on the desk and realised my mug was nowhere to be found. So, after all, I had to walk to the main building.

"Bloody, bloody, bloody ...argh. This copy machine will be the end of me." Union William cursed.

He had his performance management observation today and was already flustered. A broken copy machine was not what he needed. In fact, nobody needed a broken copy machine for two reasons. Firstly, because of the lack of textbooks due to the overlords' disregard for them, and secondly, because of the different ability levels in every class. Serfs worshipped the copy machine. It was our point of pilgrimage. Daily visits, sometimes several daily visits, would invigorate any serf or, in Union William's case, send them to the grave.

"Let me help you."

"Eva, yes, please."

I felt confident that years of fixing, kicking and stroking this machine would be the solution, and it was. William was over the moon. Nobody wanted to turn up at an observation without the necessary paperwork, including a copy of the lesson plan, the annotated seating plan, photos of the kids, the marksheet with detailed information on target levels, predictions, English as a foreign language, ethnic group, pupil premium, free school meal and young carer responsibility and other indices which would be used to create fancy and colourful charts by the likes of Mr Cunningham, the Assistant Headteacher for Curriculum and Assessment. Not having the correct paperwork meant an automatic red mark against the serf's name. Better to be prepared. There was nothing wrong with killing more trees and adding to the recycling bin's content if it meant being able to pay the bills next month.

William taught science, but physics was his speciality. Living with an Iguana pet lizard named Jojo, he made an interesting character. He spent most of his time with his niece and nephew. When he did not work, he had a great social life, attending concerts and festivals and doing a lot of additional work as the school's union representative. A role which brought him more enemies than admirers amongst the overlords. William knew all the rules by heart and was unafraid to cite them. Most kids and serfs liked this six-foot, white-headed, well-groomed guy who could teach engaging lessons on complex topics. Two minutes after having rushed off, William returned, out of breath.

"Eva, listen, don't forget the union meeting next Monday. They are coming for us."

He whispered, especially the bit on *coming for us*. He looked around with his striking blue eyes to signal they were listening too.

"I am on a trip next Monday, so I cannot make it, but I will let the others know about it," I promised.

"And good luck with the observation." I smiled whilst pouring the hot water into my mug.

I joined the union during teacher training, inspired by my lecturer at university and the fact that it was free for trainees and early career teachers. These days, it costs me nearly £20 per month, but it was money well spent. One accusation by a kid or an overlord trying to eliminate a serf for a new, cheaper worker bee could end anyone's career. I did not want this additional cloud over my head and thought better safe than sorry. I did not go to a gym or socialise much; therefore, spending this money in case a lawyer was needed was acceptable. In addition, bargaining together had more impact than bargaining alone. This was the one time I would join a team effort. The meeting on Monday, I knew already, would be about the possibility of strikes because of the workload in the factory, linked to new initiatives being implemented right, left and centre without a proper impact assessment. I was up for it.

Slowly, I walked back to my room, where Sam waited.

"Before I forget it, I just bumped into William, and he reminded me of the union meeting on Monday. Make sure you can make it."

Sam nodded.

"Yes, it's in my planner already. Workers unite."

"Workers unite," I replied.

I had referred Sam to Union William to learn about her rights and responsibilities as a serf. This was something Sam's first training school had not done, probably because union membership was frowned upon and the mentor there enjoyed being overworked. It was not part of the standard teacher training process. Still, it was part of *Eva's mentoring for a real-life programme,* together with the weekly questions about life outside the factory and the reminders to cultivate supplementary hobbies. This is how I knew about Sam's puppy and two brothers, that Sam wrote poetry in her free time and that she had just dumped her long-term boyfriend.

Life outside school was the first to suffer when people started to train as serfs, friendships ended, relationships broke up, kids resented their parents, and mental health went down the drain. I had made union knowledge and a life outside the factory compulsory for all my trainees for self-protection and self-preservation. And I was proud when they left their factory placement with me as fully-fledged union members, still holding on to interests unrelated to education. Congratulated myself on being another defender of workers' rights equipped to deal with the complexities of employment law, ready not to be mistreated.

"How is doggy?" I asked Sam.

She got her phone out, and we spent the next five minutes oohing and aahing over the little, fluffy ball that was Sam's four-month-old puppy. I grabbed a few notes, and we went to the Humanities office nearby to start Sam's weekly mentor meeting.

“Eva, last night I read this article about a guy who had called employees *human capital stock.* Can you believe this?"

"Yes, I can, and that's why I am in a union."

"What an odd phrase! Apparently, it was an

old phrase originally used to describe the level of education or skill across a workforce, but this guy used it to mean workers. That did not go down well."

"Rightly so. Human capital stock for him was probably all the employed people. They were digits on a balance sheet." I said.

"Yes, like my brother, who at 21 earns £10.18 for an hour of work."

"And now imagine doing the same job but being under 18 and getting around £5 for the same work."

"I know it's awful, isn't it?" Sam wondered, "My brother said his boss lets him know each Sunday around 10 pm when and how many hours he works the following week."

"This sounds like a chaotic nightmare. How were people meant to live on such low pay?"

"And why did those under 18 earn even less?"

"That is a good question. Last time I checked, landlords, electricity companies and supermarkets did not have different rents, charges or prices for different age groups."

"Eva, I don't think I will stay in this country. Have you heard of those crappy zero-hour contracts?"

"Some devilish invention which works in favour of the boss only. How can anyone ever plan life on a zero-hour contract? Such practices should be banned."

"Yes, if a business cannot make enough money

to pay proper wages and apply decent working conditions, it is a self-indulgent hobby, not a business. It should not exist."

"I am with you. A job is a job and should pay enough to cover the bills, and there should be no difference in pay for the same work. Those people, those bosses, those politicians and those delusional characters in society who defended this exploitation are contaminated by greed."

"They commit theft. If we walked into a shop and stole something, it would be called theft, and we would have to go to court and probably go to prison, but stealing wages was somehow acceptable." Sam said.

"Too many people built their lives on the back of the low-paid human capital stock on insecure working arrangements. Supermarket workers, delivery drivers, foreign nannies and cleaners who hold the backs of those apologists, climbing up the career ladder and drinking a cocktail after work worth two hours pay for their human capital stock."

"Yes, there is even a so-called *Low Pay Commission* to advise the government on wages."

"Well, the name says it all. I have heard they use the median wage to make recommendations. From this, smart people should know that too many people do not earn enough. Where is the outrage? Where are the marches outside Parliament contesting those wages and working conditions? Where was the noise from underpaid teenagers, parents and political parties?"

"The silence is deafening. The system is messed up when the country needs a *Low Pay Commission.*"

"You know, Sam, once you have finished your first year, I suggest you find yourself a nice factory abroad. I might do the same when Bella is a bit older."

Sam nodded and logged into the office computer to open her online portfolio while simultaneously checking her Instagram. She was on her second placement as part of her teacher training and would stay another six weeks. Her first placement was in another local factory, but as trainees, they had to experience different factories. The kids loved this 23-year-old's energy, apart from the naughty ones, because she would deal with them swiftly. We had to discuss Sam's progress towards the teacher standards and her weekly observation every Wednesday.

"Let's have a look."

Sam scrolled through her portfolio, and we stared at the screen. More than 40 standards had to be completed, and each one had to be ticked three times over the year of training to ensure they had been ticked. The eight sub-categories ranged from having high expectations of kids, over-adapting teaching to suit their needs, marking and catering to different needs and managing behaviour effectively. Those standards apply to every serf, not just the trainees. It was nothing too strange or weird, just everyday stuff, but for the newbies, it took some time before they completed the tick exercise.

However, some standards related to the personal and professional conduct of serfs. They demanded that serfs uphold public trust in the profession and maintain high standards of ethics and behaviour within and outside school. A wishy-washy kind of standard, included almost as if to trip up people because its vagueness allowed for all sorts of interpretations. How far did this stretch? I had once asked an overlord about this, and he had told me that if I got in trouble on a Saturday night out, I would probably be suspended. Now, were we not all innocent until proven guilty? I wanted to reply, but I was too shocked to say anything. Apparently, serfs were not innocent until proven guilty. They were just guilty. I never got arrested and was pretty dull regarding causing trouble on a Saturday. I did not leave the house enough to chance an arrest. It was not the fear of punishment but the need for specific details of how this standard would be applied. Any event could be interpreted in any manner depending on whoever was passing judgement. I also asked myself where these standards were for politicians. I did not find evidence of their existence.

"Sam, let's see what we can tick off this week. Are you ready for teacher bingo?"

"Born ready."

"Ok, your marking of year seven books accounts for guiding kids in reflecting on their progress because kids had to reply to your green marking and thus reflected."

Sam recorded it in her portfolio. Tick.

"Your wonderfully created writing frames for the Year 10s count as promotion of high literacy standards because you have helped students write extended essays."

Tick.

"The progress data you have already entered into the school's system smells of nothing else but using relevant data to monitor progress."

Tick again.

"Your attendance at parent's evening this week will surely be a tick in the box for communicating effectively with parents, but you have to save this one for next week because the parents' evening does not happen until later today."

"Agreed. We can not record the future in this portfolio."

"Correct, especially as history teachers."

Because Sam was super organised, my job was made easier. She had nearly completed each standard three times during training requirements, and I was proud of her. Sam would make a first-rate teacher, and she would not take nonsense from any overlords either.

"Eva, can you help me with risk assessments please?" Sam turned towards me.

"Let's do this now."

I opened the blank risk assessment on the factory's system and another one I had completed last June before I took a group of kids to Duxford for a day at the Imperial War Museum.

"Whenever you organise a trip and leave the factory premises, you must complete a risk assessment, and in some circumstances, even when on site."

"What is it I have to do? Do I actually have to go to the place?"

"The sad answer is yes. You will spend your day off to go there. So it's worth considering taking kids to places you enjoy."

"Makes sense." Sam nodded.

"Last time I went to Duxford, I looked for dangers and thought up crazy ideas of what could go wrong," I explained, "You really have to put yourself in the shoes of a teenager."

"Wow, I must employ mental acrobatics to imagine any eventuality."

"That's accurate. Think about all the crazy things kids may get up to, like climbing into one of the planes, falling the steps upwards, jumping on or off something, hurting themselves or others, including members of the public."

Sam took notes.

"Also, keep in mind any terrorists who might attack a museum and consider the risks associated with the coach breaking down en route."

"I am not sure I ever want to organise a trip," Sam said, looking concerned, "It's too much extra work on the weekend."

"You are right, but it is important for insurance purposes because a too-risky risk means kids have to stay at the factory."

"Do parents think of all this before taking their kids anywhere?" Sam wanted to know.

"As a serf and parent, I can tell you the answer is no. It is crazy that as a serf, I pay more attention to other people's kids than my own. A hazard that comes with the job. Maybe also because our kids had it already drilled into them to hold on to our hand, to stay near us, to wait or to look out for us," I laughed," Our kids are equipped with phone numbers in pockets, special wristbands with parents' details simply because they are teacher kids."

"It sounds like every trip for them is a school trip with packed lunches and learning activities. These teacher kids know the drill." Sam added.

"Yes, they were institutionalised before they even entered an institution. Poor, lucky little ones," I said, " For risk assessments, you must stretch your imagination further than normal life. Put yourself in the shoes of a kid who has experienced very little primary socialisation and was now heavily influenced by peers who are full of hormones and not so full of reasoning and intelligent decision making."

"And once I have walked around the museum, unpaid, I must complete this form?" Sam pointed at the form open on the screen.

"Exactly."

"Has this always happened?" she wanted to know.

"I had no idea when this became the norm, but back in my day, we had a mathematics teacher who announced in the middle of the lesson that we would all take a trip to the supermarket five minutes away to measure the cartons of milk and to work out whether one litre really fitted into them or the milk companies were lying. I can guarantee you, this man had no risk assessment."

"No way. What did your parents say?"

"Nothing. It was normal. We loved it," I continued, " Mr Potis, the man who took 28 kids into a supermarket by himself without a risk assessment, without asking permission from the head teacher, the parents or anyone, just decided in the middle of the lesson that this would be the best way to teach us. And this is how we found ourselves in the fridge aisles in the supermarket near the school measuring cartons, working out the capacity."

"Wow, that could never happen today."

Sam was fascinated.

"Mr Potis could sign on at the job centre if he pulled such a stunt now," I replied.

Back then, another era was tucked away in my memory, buried like a history book, dusty and in old print which nobody could read anymore. A dead era in a dead country.

"Let me email you this Duxford version for reference."

Sam and I agreed to another lesson observation for next Tuesday. We were about to finish the meeting when Joanna walked past the open office door, her shoulders moving up as she sobbed hard. I jumped out of my seat.

"Joanna, come here. What happened?"

I pulled her into the little office, shutting the door behind us. Joanna could not contain herself. Under heavy breathing, she was speaking, but we were unable to comprehend. Sam stroked Joanna's back, and I handed Joanna a tissue.

"Would you like a cup of tea?"

Joanna nodded, tears streaming down her face. She sat on a pile of textbooks which had been banned by the overlords and were collecting dust in the corner.

While Sam worked on the tea, I sat on the dusty floor before Joanna.

"Joanna, what happened."

She started to calm down.

"Adil, you know, Adil in Year 9?"

I nodded. Everyone knew Adil.

"He threw a planner in my face."

I could see a red line across her nose and lips. Adil, no more comment was necessary. He had been excluded several times for violence against both kids and staff. Still, he somehow managed to return to the factory floor, avoiding permanent exclusion and making life miserable for all who encountered him.

"Is someone in your class right now?" I asked.

"Yes, Cunningham took over," Joanna replied with her hands around her cup of tea.

"What would you like to do next?"

"I want to go home, see my GP and get signed off. I think I am breaking down. I cannot do this any longer."

This was not the first time Adil had wrecked her lesson even though she had asked the Head of Year, the head of the department and the overlords for support and help. Nothing had materialised, and she was left alone to deal with a young offender in her class whilst trying to teach everyone else a good lesson.

"Let's go and get your things."

Together, Joanna and I walked to the staffroom to get her jacket. After that, Joanna quickly spoke to her line manager to report what had happened and to let him know that she would be going home and seeing her GP. Mr Tracer, the overlord in charge of Teaching and Learning, needed clarification as to why Joanna wanted to go home in the first place and did not see the point of her contacting the GP. He was clearly confused.

"Will you be back for tonight's parents' evening?"

"Probably not."

Mr Tracer looked shocked and was speechless. I took Joanna by the arm and walked her into the car park.

"Listen, Missy, go to your GP, get signed off and write down all the incidents that have occurred. Also, go back through your emails, save everything Adil-related, and contact your union."

Joanna nodded, got into her car and was not seen for the rest of the term.

I raced back to Sam in the office, and we both were silent and shocked about what happened.

"And this is why we need to be in unions."

"Absolutely."

"Ok, Sam, soon all the standards will be ticked, and you can call yourself an early career teacher. I was called a newly qualified teacher in old money, but whatever you will be called does not matter because you are awesome. See you later."

"See you, Eva, and thank you." Sam walked off in the opposite direction.

I could not help but think back to my teacher training when there was no online portfolio. Every standard had to be documented on paper and evidence attached. The portfolio was handed to our professional tutor at the university at the end of June. The standard joke in our group was that nobody would look at the folder, but universities would just weigh it, and if it were heavy enough, we would pass.

During my teacher training in North London, my university lecturer walked up and down the classroom each lecture and referred to us as *guys, you guys will do this, and you guys will experience that.* I liked Mrs Jonas, a former hippie who was very knowledgeable on all things teaching related, unions, social mobility, or lack of it. She wrote for newspapers and social justice groups. Her lectures were relaxed and engaging.

I was lucky with my teacher trainee group, too. It was an exciting bunch of people. Some were in their early twenties, straight out of university, and others, like me, from abroad. Some already had distinguished careers before deciding to educate the next generation. They had been journalists and bankers. Nearly all of the trainees from my cohort of 25 stayed in teaching after their training. Considering the annual teacher exodus, most have probably found new careers by now. The papers keep telling us that 50% of early career teachers considered leaving the profession within the first five years.

Like Sam, I had to go to two different secondary factories, both inner-city factories. And twice, I won the jackpot with my mentors. They were approachable and had their act together. The one thing I did not like during her teacher training was the week-long placement in a primary factory. Everything took much longer and was much higher pitched, and the days bored me. However, it also made me admire primary factory serfs even more because I would not have had the patience to deal with those little people. Teaching someone to read, write, and do simple maths required far more patience than teaching kids how to write an essay about the Cold War.

My mentors had lives outside the factory. They cared about the kids but also set boundaries to protect their sanity. I understood why politicians did not want to send their kids to this establishment where I trained. It made sense that parents rejected this factory. Having worked in this purgatory for twelve weeks, I contemplated what type of illegal work I could do should Bella ever have to go to a factory resembling anything like this one. Who wanted their kid walking out of school with a knife in their head? It was not the serfs. The system, the environment, and society in general had let this factory down. Some believe things would improve by changing the name and replacing the old overlords with a fresh set of box tickers. And things usually did get better. On paper. Not in reality. The system could be manipulated. I had experienced it first-hand. I did not trust inspection reports, having seen the random allocation of grades and how some places manoeuvred the inspection days. All but one of the schools I had ever worked at removed the hard-core offenders when the inspectors appeared. Suddenly, those kids were on trips or, worse, hidden in rooms with teaching assistants far away from the prying eye of the torturers. Whatever I heard about any factory, I took it not with a pinch but a truckload of salt.

Due to teacher shortages, my mentor in my second placement school was also a trainee like me. This graduate scheme trainee, who went on to establish a think tank, and I, had to look after each other and the kids. We were both thrown into the deep end, but we were competent swimmers, supporting each other in this factory that had seen its fair share of tragedy. Although smaller, the problems were as enormous as in my first placement factory. This time around, I felt like a social worker. The prayer at the start of lessons calmed kids for five minutes, but prayer alone could not overcome the social problems faced by many of the kids living across the road from one of the wealthiest areas in the country. To stay sane, I had to remind myself that this was just a job and all the kids had parents or carers. I could never, not even by working 24 hours instead of thirteen or fourteen, change every child's circumstance or undo the damage the rest of society had already done. All I could do was teach and make the 60 minutes with me as good a learning event as possible.

WEDNESDAY, 1 PM

I promised to work with Jo and Lucy on essay writing skills for their Politics A-level exam in a few days. Their predicted grades were less rosy than universities would like, but they were determined to get there. They also wanted to avoid being withdrawn from the exams just days before the event. A little tactic employed not only by private factories but more and more common in the state factory sector is to keep results in line with expectations. The windows needed dressing for OFSTED's ever-moving goalposts. Having wasted the first 18 months of their A-levels talking in lessons, not completing any homework, and, according to their admission, generally being lazy, they had realised by January that a certain amount of work was actually required to get the grades needed to get into any university. I had seen huge improvements in their work since their enlightenment, and I wanted them to succeed. That is how I found myself in my room during lunch with two teenage girls and a massive pile of diabetes-inducing snacks to compare the US and UK

Supreme Court.

Jo, an avid swimmer, spent most of her time in the pool, whether this was before or after school or at weekends. She was swimming at the nationals and had finally applied her willingness to work hard, which she had for swimming, to her academic studies. Lucy, equally as sporty but from a cash-stricken family, had to give up on her dream to compete because her parents could not afford the fees for coaches. We will never know how far she could have gone. Money makes the world go around; her family did not have it. So, here she was. For her, the earth did not move.

"Miss, do you think the American kids know all this about the US Supreme Court?" Jo asked.

"I don't know, but the point is that you need to know all this next week."

Lucy complained, "How is this fair? I am not even American."

"But you chose this A level."

"Miss, but why can't they do anything fun?"

"Over the years of teaching, I have gotten the impression that the exams are not meant to be fun," I said, "Now, let's start with the structure. What goes in the introduction, Jo?"

I could tell that Jo had done her revision, she rattled down the points for the introduction and continued with the other paragraphs as well. Lucy listened attentively and scribbled down notes. The girls managed to plan the whole essay and discuss what needed to go into each paragraph, including recent Supreme Court rulings, to show the examiner that they had paid attention to the news. By the time lunch was nearly over, they had written half of their essay, promised to complete the rest tonight and emailed me their answers. With that agreed, they set off to their next lesson. I was high on sugar and caffeine. My hands shook, and my heart beat faster than an average afternoon. This unofficial payment for tuition was welcome but had an impact on my energy levels.

I waited outside for Hoodie Boy's class and heard them before I saw them. Some kids tried to hide behind the bike shed; others walked in the wrong direction. They could no longer hide in the toilets because they would be locked after break and lunch. Creativity was needed to find new hiding spots. Upcoming exams could have made them walk faster. In fact, many kids hoped that by attending any of the after-school revision sessions offered by most serfs for free, they could cram the content and skills into their brains at the last minute. Exam content osmosis was a dangerous undertaking. It did not occur to them that they had already been taught all this content in their regular lessons, but they had chosen not to listen.

After 15 minutes of dribs and drabs, all year

11s were in the room apart from, surprise, surprise, Hoodie Boy. He was somewhere on site; I knew this because I had spotted him earlier, and from the register, I could see that he had been in all day. I was glad he had not made it yet. At least I could start the lesson, and maybe we would get what I had planned.

Beep. Beep. Beep. Beep.

Laughter and fake panic noises arose. Not today. We do not have time for this. The year 11s approached this alarm sound with the same urgency as they approached their usual lessons or exams without any urgency. Our outbuilding was not on fire, so why bother walking quickly to the field to line up with the class alphabetically in a single file, only to be shouted at by a Head of Year or the overlords?

"Guys, let's move to the field. "

I was a shepherd without a sheepdog and a herd that found all this amusing.

"Go to your form groups and line up," I said whilst more than a thousand people crawled out of the building towards the sports field.

It took nearly ten minutes for all of them to be outside. Clearly, there was no fire anywhere on site. The scheduled drills were known to staff, and nothing had been announced this morning during the overlords' daily show. It could be concluded that this kid had pressed the fire alarm as part of their avoidance strategy, or there was a tiny likelihood of the food tech department burning cookies. The more plausible explanation was a false alarm initiated by a prankster at work.

I went to my form group, who had already found their line on the sports field. My teacher's stare was enough to get them in line. They still felt guilty over the porn incident, even though all but two were innocent, and thus most of them behaved like little angels and the register was taken in no time. Nobody had gone missing in the pretend fire, and nobody was hurt either. At least it was May, and the warm sun shone on our faces. I appreciated standing in the fresh air and feeling the sun's rays on my cheeks. Fire drills or fake alarms were more annoying in winter and even worse in the rain.

An eternity later, Mrs Viper, having been told by the factory's overlords and Head of Year underlings that all was good, declared that it was time to return to class. Like ants on a mission, people moved in different directions.

Beep. Beep. Beep. Beep.

We had just arrived back in our room when the alarm started again, and the whole procedure had to be repeated. This time, it took longer to settle the swarm of humans. There was more shouting on the teachers' side and more laughing, giggling and general silliness on the kids' side. Mrs Viper was clearly annoyed, and her underlings looked worried. Who of them was to blame for this misfortune? Why did the alarm keep going off? Was there an Assistant Headteacher for Fire Drills? The overlords kept talking on their walkie-talkies until Mr Sullivan approached Mrs Viper and whispered in her ear.

I watched all this while waiting for my form group. The overlords had probably worked out who or what had manipulated the fire alarm. They likely had someone in their mind who kept sending the factory population back onto the field. With my love for crime shows, I had already created an offender profile that pinpointed who was responsible for this sabotage. It looked very much like Hoodie Boy, who was clearly at school but had not ended up in my lesson. CCTV cameras would later confirm my suspicion, and Hoodie Boy would be found guilty, just as I had predicted with my forensic skills. Maybe a career in the FBI was still possible for me. Only a little would happen, though. An after-school detention was all they could punish him with. By the time the alarm drama was finally over, we had 15 minutes left. Hoodie Boy never appeared. Good. This meant I was able to teach almost uninterrupted. This mattered, especially with the sound of exams knocking on the factory's door.

My last lesson of the day was with the Year 12s. They were in their first year of a subject they had chosen. Apart from the regicide, the Stuarts and the Civil Wars were not the most exciting topics, but they had to be studied. I liked this keen group. There were only 14 kids in the class, and most were interested. There was not one Hoodie Boy-type character, which was a bonus. They just turned up, mostly did a pretty decent job and went to their next lesson. By the end of the lesson, my blood sugar had not yet stabilised from the Jo and Lucy diabetes session.

WEDNESDAY, 3:45 PM

"Nazma, I am starving, do you know whether they have put out the sandwiches for parents' evening yet?"

"You do not want to eat those poisonous stale sandwiches, do you?" Namza said with a disgusted look on her face.

"Not really, but I have to stay here till seven tonight, and my body is in starvation alert mode."

Nazma smiled and took my hand.

"Come with me. I do not want you to be sick tomorrow, so I have some goodies in the learning support area."

I followed without asking any further questions because I knew if Nazma had goodies, they would be divine, and those sandwiches from the cheapest supplier without much in them could be fed to someone else. We arrived in the learning support unit on the outskirts of the factory's premises, which was good because the overlords found this location too far away from their paradise and would only come here sometimes.

Nazma opened the green front door to the run-down unit with the formerly white walls, and it smelled like some five-star Asian restaurant. She led me straight to a heavy, silver pot which could have fed 15 people. She took a paper plate.

"Sit down. You need to be fed."

She filled this plate with one of my favourite dishes. I was given a huge mountain of chicken biryani and a plastic fork. I thought I had died and gone to food heaven.

"Nazma, thank you so much for this. You are a lifesaver. When are you starting your restaurant?"

"I made this last night because many of us have to stay here tonight to translate, so I thought, why not make a small biryani."

"A small biryani? This is so delicious. That is exactly what I needed today."

Amongst the teaching assistants and learning mentors who were still busy phoning parents, helping students and preparing resources, I nearly fell into a food coma. What a great meal. Some of the teaching assistants joined me. They had been asked to stay behind their normal hours. They were needed. Many parents without sufficient English skills would arrive, and the teaching assistant had excellent language skills and translated for the parents. Sometimes, they were so busy that children had to translate for their parents. For some, this was an embarrassing experience. Those kids almost took on the role of the parent, having to explain what was happening at school and how things worked in the system rather than the parents leading the way. Not only was it uncomfortable for some, but it was also a problem when the somewhat more naughty children did the translating for their parents and left out the critical pieces of information on their behaviour in lessons or the lack of independent learning.

"Hey, how are you?" Agata walked over and sat down next to me.

"Agata, thank you. Right now, I feel amazing, have you tried this awesome biryani?"

"Not yet, but I have to."

"Thank you so much for dealing with Sunjit yesterday, removing him from the classroom and contacting the Head of Year. "

"No worries, what was he thinking? These kids, seriously. If he said this in front of his parents, they would both have a heart attack. Imagine."

"You are right. I met his father yesterday. He was here by lunch and kept apologising. I think he really felt bad," I said, "Come over to mine over half-term. I owe you."

"I am here for the first weekend, and then I am going to Portugal for the rest of the half-term, so let's do the first Saturday, what do you think?"

"Great, I will cook."

"And I will bring the vodka." Agata winked.

"It's a deal."

It was time to get ready. I checked my phone and had already received a message from Azma saying Bella was fine. Azma often offered to take Bella to her house on her parents' evenings. I was grateful for this. Without family in this country and with the baby's father being rather useless in parenting, I relied on people such as Azma or Ajinder, who also sometimes looked after Bella. I quickly replied to Azma. Then I grabbed the data sheets for Year 10's parents' evening and this night's marking because as soon as the evening shift was over, I wanted to escape without returning to my room.

At least, in this factory, these public relation exercises always started at 4.30 pm, and I would be home by 8 pm. I had 32 appointments, which was not too bad, not too good either. Jeremy's mum, who was a probation officer, complained that she worked with offenders and murderers, but she could not get her son out of bed in the morning. What was there to do? Abdul's mum could not get him off the PlayStation. He just would not study. What was there to do? Sophia's dad told me about her being on the phone all day and night. What was there to do? I was here to talk about targets, predictions, and strategies for my subject, and I knew the answer. I knew what there was to do. It was called parenting. Start to parent. That was what there was to do. Start being a parent. Start being an adult in this relationship. I wanted to be blunt and honest and say what needed to be said. Drag Jeremy out of bed in the morning, take Abdul's PlayStation away, confiscate Sophia's phone, and change the wifi password. Please just do something. I was frustrated by all this. I was blamed for kids not reaching targets, even though my teaching was apparently deemed outstanding. I worried about my performance management targets, my job security and how to pay my bills. Yet, here I was surrounded by parents who could not do what was necessary for their children to revise and study at home.

I snapped out of my little sorry cloud back into this collection of parents.

"Fatima, I cannot speak to you about your brother. You are in year 11, and he is in year 10. Where are your mum and dad?"

Fatima smiled.

“My mum is home with my baby brother, and my dad has to work tonight."

"OK, I will call your parents tomorrow and talk to them directly about Junaid. Thank you for coming. Bye."

Trying to send an older sibling when they were in the same school was a trick some parents tried to pull. It baffled me. Did the parents not want to know about their child's progress at the factory? I made a note of calling Junaid's parents tomorrow. This added to my workload and was unpaid, of course. They had been given an appointment for tonight. What a waste of time.

Laila's mum sat down with pen and paper, wanting to know which books to buy, which websites to use and how to help Laila, who was already a top kid. I wanted to cry. Laila's mum was a single parent and turned up on time to every parents' evening despite working full-time. Where were all those Laila's parents? We need more Laila parents, I thought. This evening went pretty quickly, and I could hardly catch my breath. By 7.30 pm, I got up, took my bags and left the factory door as quickly as possible. Having given three hours of my life to discuss problems of parenting rather than education, I had to engage in the parenting business myself.

WEDNESDAY, 7:35 PM

There will be no more parents' evenings this academic year. They would start again in October, along with other public relations exercises such as open evenings, when parents and kids had the chance to look around their chosen factory, which, for the show night, looked like a Disney Castle. There was always a lot of singing and dancing, silly activities that would never happen on a regular school day, but the show had to go on. They served lies, and everyone knew it. Everyone would eventually go home and pretend all was good, but it was not. Months later, in March, the crocodile tears would rain, and friendships threatened to split over factory decisions made by local authorities. Panic would set in amongst parents because their child was not meant to go to a factory where knives were routinely carried. A child's postcode determined their factory place and whether they carried a knife, a book, or both. Frantic appeals would keep secondary factories busy until after the new academic year had already started.

Azma only lived five minutes from our place, and there was hardly any traffic then. I grabbed the box of chocolates I had bought as a little thank you and rang the bell of the terraced house with the small front garden. Inside, I heard Bella and Hafsah giggling. Azma opened the door with a huge smile.

"Hey Eva, how was your evening? Are you hungry?"

"Hey Azma, all went well. No, I am not hungry. Thank you. How are you? How were the girls?"

Around the corner came Bella and Hafsah with some Bollywood-inspired dance routines.

"Mami, Mami, look, we learnt this dance."

Bella was excited to show off her moves. Together, the girls dragged me into the living room, each holding one of my hands.

"Sit down and watch, please, Mami," Bella begged.

Azma nodded encouragingly and returned with a cup of tea a few minutes later.

"Ah, thank you, Azma. Here are some chocolates for you. I hope you like them."

I handed Azma the chocolate and took the tea while the girls repeatedly performed the same moves.

"Girls, I really love your dance routine. Maybe Bella can teach me at home. Sadly, for today, we need to go. Bella, please say thank you to Azma."

I had to end the fun for tonight.

"Azma, thank you for having me."

"Bella, you are welcome in our house any time."

WEDNESDAY, 8:45 PM

"Mami, can I teach you our dance tonight?"

"No, Baby Bella, it is bedtime, and I have work. How about tomorrow?"

"Hm, ok." Bella was disappointed.

"Please get ready for bed and brush your teeth."

Bella walked to the bathroom slowly, but three seconds later, she ran back past me, opened her school bag and pulled out a ball of paper.

"Mami, Mami, look what I got."

I wanted to scream. It was a food technology ingredients list for a carrot cake. The kids needed the items by tomorrow morning. Why did factories hand this out so late? I mentally ticked some items I knew we had at home off the list, but we did not have carrots, sultanas, or margarine.

"Ten, nine, eight, seven, breathe ...one."

I needed to calm down.

"Well, Baby Bella, it looks like we have to abort

bedtime for now and jump back into the car."

She seemed to like the idea of leaving the house around bedtime. Her huge grin gave her away.

Bella ran ahead into the 24-hour Tescos, all excited. I followed with far less enthusiasm. I was tired and wanted to prepare for my lesson observation. And as day followed night, as soon as we entered the consumer ball, the year eight twins, Shazi and Rabia, waved excitedly.

"Miss, Miss, what are you doing here?"

I don't know, looking for a new job was my preferred answer, but I had to uphold professionalism and respect for the profession at all times, even outside school. Bella was not yet in university, so I needed the job for a little while longer to pay the bills. I also bit my tongue as their father kept following me around the supermarket, trying to talk to me, not about his kids but my private life. He was undeterred by me saying *goodbye* several times over, nor was he bothered that Bella was next to me. What a creep. I got away from him by talking to Bella and walking faster. The stalker's dad gave up after around ten minutes, and we continued our shopping in peace.

The goodies created in tomorrow's Masterchef session will be in the bin. This was a given. I did not eat anything made in primary factories with sticky fingers and snotty noses. Bella, of course, would never be allowed to know this. I had to waste money buying content for the bin whilst trying to keep my job by staying professional in the face of a stalker.

We found everything on the list and decided that expensive doughnuts were needed to reward ourselves. As we went to one of the tills furthest from the main entrance, I noticed a boy who looked just like Hoodie Boy. No way. I deliberated, he had probably half the shop in his trousers, which still hung under his butt. I realised he was there with two smaller kids when I came closer. The younger one, probably four, was crying; he looked tired and the older one, a girl who was late primary factory age, looked sad too. And yes, it was Hoodie Boy. He looked flustered. He had not noticed me.

"That's £15.64, please, cash or card."

Hoodie Boy, looking for something in his pockets whilst trying to calm the crying four-year-old, stuttered, "Oh, sorry, I think I must have, I think my money is at home. I am sorry, I think I must come back tomorrow."

He took the already-packed items from the carrier bag and placed them near the cashier.

I watched this scene and encountered a Hoodie Boy I had never seen before, a human. I noticed human suffering. There he was, this tough guy *with ladies in the Hilton* looking after what I now assumed was his two younger siblings, and he had left his money at home.

"No worries. I will pay for this."

On hearing this hoodie, the boy turned around and realised it was me, his boring history teacher. The woman who had sent for an overlord only yesterday to get him removed.

"Thank you, but you really do not have to do this. I can come back tomorrow." He whispered.

This was the first time I had heard him say something in a normal voice, without aggression and threat.

"It's no problem, Mikhail. I will pay for it. Are they your siblings?" I nodded towards the younger ones.

"Yes, Miss. My mum is in hospital, and my dad is working late, so I had to bring them with me."

I smiled and got my card out to pay for Mikhail's shopping.

"Thank you, Miss. I will return the money tomorrow."

He grabbed the bag, put it in his trolley and carried his little brother in his arms down the aisle towards the exit with his sister following, waving at us.

Bella watched this scene unfold in silence.

"Mama, is this one of your kids? Why did he have no money, and why did he have no parents?"

"Yes, he is one of my kids, and he has parents, but they were busy, so he had to look after his siblings."

I wondered why his mum was in the hospital and what type of job the father had. I had never seen his parents on parents' evenings. I also hoped this cashier would not attempt to talk to me. I refused to be hostage to small talk. The worst offenders of this pseudo-talk were found right here in supermarket queues and on public transport. No, I did not want to share how my day was. No, I was not interested in what someone would be cooking tonight. No, I did not care where someone was going. I just wanted to be in places, in silence. Left alone.

"£21.89, please, cash or card?" the cashier interrupted my thought.

"Card, please."

I felt guilty for thinking Hoodie Boy was causing trouble in the supermarket when he had to look after small kids. It was already late, and the little one must have been tired. I hoped that he and the younger kids got home alright.

"Come on, baby Bella, let's have those doughnuts."

On the way out, I grabbed the box of doughnuts from the trolley and handed it to Bella.

"Mami, the peanut butter ones are my favourites."

"I know, baby, let me have one of the sugar-glazed ones."

Munching, we walked to the car, got in and drove home. Mission accomplished, I pondered whilst driving and watching Bella in the rear mirror, smiling and indulging in her doughnut. All ingredients had been acquired, a young boy's evening had been saved, and there were a few more doughnuts to eat. All in all, it was a great end to a chaotic night.

After Bella had gone to bed, I finally sat down to complete the preparations for my lesson observation, including marking the exercise books of the group I would be seen with. Unlike Sam, who was a trainee and was seen every week, once serfs survived their first two full years in a factory, we would be seen three times a year to ensure our teaching was still up to scratch. Three times a year, I and my fellow serfs were close to a nervous breakdown. This was like a mini-inspection that could spell the end of a teacher's career or at least the end of working in a particular factory. No matter how good someone was in this teaching business, overlords would find ways to move that face along if the face did not fit.

I always had full-blown anxiety in the days leading up to these inspections, but they had to happen as part of teacher appraisal or performance management, as it was called in the more business-like factories. No matter how often I told myself that I knew how to teach, no matter that my observations had always gone smoothly and my colleagues and the overlords thought I had understood teaching, I was always a wreck.

I created the PowerPoint a few days ago and prepared all the activities. I still needed to complete the differentiated worksheets, the Polish version and the new arrival version. I also had to type my lesson plan, colour-code the seating plan and quickly prepare some more questions according to Bloom's taxonomy.

It was nearly midnight before I reached bed, but I could not get much sleep. The observation weighed heavily on me, and to add to that, I had an appointment with Bella's headteacher before school.

THURSDAY, 5:12 AM

Anxiety was my alarm clock on an observation day. No gadget was required to shock me into a state of heightened alert. I woke up too early but could not fall back asleep and decided to sit with my coffee in the kitchen, staring at the wall and listening to the humming of the fridge until it was time to start the day, by which time I felt exhausted. It was also election day. I had spent over £1300 on my British citizenship, so I wanted to use my right to vote. I looked forward to showing Bella how voting worked. Teachers' kids were forever learning. Like their parents, teacher kids were not allowed a break.

On the way to the breakfast club, Bella seemed preoccupied, and suddenly, tears streamed down her face.

"What's up, baby? What happened?"

Bella choked and, after a few seconds, revealed her perceived crime.

"I forgot my literacy homework on the kitchen table at home."

"Oh dear baby, no worries. Let me tell you

a secret for free. Your teacher knows that you always do your homework," I tried to sound cheerful, " When you walk up to him just before the lesson and tell him that you forgot your homework, but you will hand it in tomorrow, what do you think is the worst that can happen?"

"A detention."

"Exactly."

"The worst thing that will happen is a detention. Even that is unlikely. If it happens, you just sit there and read a book. You can bring your literacy task tomorrow, okay?"

I thought it was stupid to give detentions, especially in primary factories. Who had visualised that it would be an efficient use of a teacher's time to sit during a break, lunch or worse, after school with kids when we had so much real work? Bella looked only half-convinced, but the tears had dried. I kissed her on the cheek and dropped her off.

THURSDAY, 8:03 AM

I had to rush over to see Bella's headteacher. Her retired grandparents wanted to take her to Austria for a holiday in term-time. A permission slip was required. Mr Hammond, who with his grey hair, glasses and serious stare would not have looked out of place in an investment bank or TV studio, was another overlord who probably had a high-vis and walkie-talkie hidden somewhere. His office, a combination of brown and metallic-looking furniture, was spacious.

"Good morning, how are you?" he asked formally.

"I am fine, thank you. How about you?" I asked without being interested.

"I am well, thank you. Have a seat, please." He pointed to the seat opposite him.

I was nervous and annoyed. With my bag on my lap, I sat in the chair like a granny on the bus. Asking for permission for Bella to have a week off seemed ludicrous, given that I knew how much time was wasted in factories for behaviour management, assemblies, registration time, and waiting for someone to be quiet. The ridiculousness of this procedure would soon unfold. Mr Hammond appeared organised. It was very likely that his PA had printed the documents in front of him. It was also very likely that he had a wife who kept his home and kids in order. Bella's spotless attendance record was on the desk.

"How can I help you?" he asked, although he already knew what this was about.

"Bella's grandparents want to take Bella to Austria for five days. I would like to apply for a leave of absence for her."

My heart beat faster from anxiety and anger about what he would say, even though I knew I would ignore it anyway.

"I cannot grant this request as holidays during term time are not permitted."

I was familiar with government rules and attendance targets. However, I also knew that Bella would be in Austria with or without a permission slip from this overlord. I would call Bella's factory and excuse her for five consecutive days. First, it was a headache, and later, it developed into a full-blown stomach bug with puking and all. I had already booked the flights months ago. Nothing would stop Bella. This little meeting here was just another box-ticking exercise.

"Hm, is there no way," I asked, "Bella's grandma is a retired teacher. She will make sure Bella will complete all her work."

"Maybe if a family member was ill, I could grant such permission."

This man was capable of realism.

"Well, yes, Bella's auntie is in hospital." I declared, nodding.

"Then I can grant permission for an absence."

The newsreader smiled emotionlessly. He probably felt satisfied, knowing he could now tick all the necessary boxes. His factory's records remained as spotless as Bella's. Everyone was happy. It was a win-win. He took note of the decision on Bella's attendance record. We said goodbyes and parted ways. Stupid, nonsensical comedy! We wasted ten minutes to achieve something clear from the outset. This game had played out well, and I felt lighter walking back to the car. I saw Bella smiling and talking to the other kids through the window. The homework drama was already forgotten and would likely play out just like the request for a holiday. I sat in the car for two minutes, just watching Bella.

The drive to the factory took me through a residential area. I had time to observe the Magic Carpet Kids. Small creatures who appeared to hover just above the ground on scooters. As if by magic, they moved from their residence to an educational institution and back. It was astonishing. They did not even have to operate their magic carpets. They had someone subcontracted for this. This someone was the mother mule who pulled their magic carpet, carried their bags and sometimes even pushed another little human in a buggy. The occasional dad would tend to message and read an article on their phone whilst absentmindedly pulling along a Magic Carpet Kid. They would not notice if a kid went missing, and they would probably take the wrong kid to the factory. Had the scooter been used unaided, rather than being pulled along by a mother mule or ghost father, motor development and exercise would have been less of a problem for this generation of kids.

"Are you ready for another day in paradise?" Ajinder shouted over the roof of her beaten Audi.

"Wish me luck, it's my observation."

"No worries, you have got this. I believe in you. Which group is it with?"

"It's year 8," I replied, "they are usually fine, but we never know. Have you voted already?"

"Of course. It's all done. Come on, let's rock this boat."

Together, we walked in, waving at Flora in reception, who was already shopping on Amazon.

THURSDAY, 8:50 AM

My form group, and I had to go on a little excursion to the assembly hall to experience the joys of *collective worship*. In most factories, these weekly meetings saw a whole year group compressed into a bigger room or the hall, listening to a speech on any of those days that had been declared essential by whatever organisation was shouting the loudest. Occasionally, an ex-student turned up and talked about how they became a fighter pilot. Once a year, the guide dog organisation brought doggies to the factory. That was always my favourite assembly. The assemblies I detested the most took place in September and July. The first assembly of the year was usually dedicated to exam results and expectations. The younger kids in Year 7 had to stare at slides filled with photos of the overlords arranged in hierarchical order. They needed to understand from the outset who was who and how important these people were. In July, we all had to survive the so-called celebration assembly. It was possible to reverse the global warming trend just by eliminating those endless paper certificates handed out that day. Death due to boredom could be avoided by abolishing celebration assemblies altogether. The only people to enjoy them were tiny kids, the occasional helicopter parent, and the overlords. At the secondary factory level, they were hideous and lasted forever. Some factories made a point of having a two-hour mock version before the event. Everyone got some sort of certificate. To prepare the kids for real life, everyone was a winner. Cynical sarcasm.

The only professionals who indulged in awards ceremonies were artists, actors, and singers, who were already overpaid and pampered. They regularly showed up for self-glorification, self-congratulation and self-celebration sessions. Real people went to work outside the glitter cloud, got paid, and went home. No celebration ever.

Kids who worked hard would, by year 5, have figured out that the assemblies were a sham and utterly pointless. Along with certificates for attendance, they belonged in the bin. Nothing was remarkable about celebrating sick kids coming into the factory and spreading diseases to everyone else. Attendance certificates were distributed to those who had made it into the factory over 95 % of the time. This percentage was the government's attendance target. The system did not care about the reasons for absenteeism. Not attending school was a sin. Parents could find themselves fined or, worse, sent to prison.

Interestingly, private factories had around four more weeks of holidays per year, yet when a state factory kid did not attend for four weeks, their parents were forced to pay a fine. I had seen overlords refuse to write references for colleges on the grounds of limited school attendance, even in cases where kids still achieved top grades despite being ill all the time or refusing to attend for other reasons, such as being bullied. Assemblies wasted several lessons in themselves, but because they happened on school grounds, they did not count as absences. Learning did not take place.

Mr Josiah was in charge of today's entertainment. The topic was the General Election. I was excited about this one, evidenced by my 28 kids lined up first. They were still on perfect behaviour after the porn lesson. They did not want me to have another headache, which I appreciated. Mrs Slump, in her Birkenstocks, wobbled over to check ties, top buttons and untucked shirts as kids walked into the hall and took their seats. It was vital because Mrs Viper would be in attendance. Mr Josiah should have been on stage to prepare the kids for Mrs Viper's big entrance, but he was not where he was meant to be. There was nothing on the screen either. Nor was there any music. None of the expectations had been ticked - this spelt disaster.

I turned around, and there was Mr Josiah at the back of the assembly hall, flustered and nervously walking towards Ted and John, the IT technicians. Ted and John only came as a pair. The Siamese twins of the IT world. Where there was one, there was the other. Ted resembled a penguin with his pot belly and thick glasses. The bald 52-year-old was as calm as a monk. John, who was probably 20 years younger than Ted and a full-blown IT geek with his own YouTube channel, looked like a goth. He was nearly 6 feet tall and an avid gamer who could often be found at music festivals with his singer-girlfriend.

I knew that Mr Josiah was panicking because that was what we serfs would do if we were in the same situation. Also, he was not holding his green super slush container. It stood unsupervised on the stage. Fumbling with his notes, he waited next to Ted and John, walking around in small circles, eyes fixated on the screen. They were working to fix whatever the issue was. An assembly without a slideshow was much more challenging to present. I knew this and started feeling a bit sorry for Mr Josiah. Nobody wanted their day to start like this, especially with Mrs Viper lurking around the corner. But Ted and John were not only the Siamese Twins but also the A team of IT, and within a few minutes, they had found a solution to the problem. The words *General Election* appeared on the screen. Mr Josiah grew three inches taller. He shook Ted's and then John's hand, thanking them, and walked up on stage with energetic steps. The morning had been saved, and everything was nearly ready for the empress of doom.

Mr Josiah projected his voice into every corner of the hall.

"Good morning, students. Please stand for Mrs Viper."

The empress slithered into the hall, looking right and left, scanning kids and teachers like she did every morning in briefings. She sat in her allocated seat next to an unfortunate kid who did not move for the rest of the assembly. Mr Josiah's assembly went smoothly. The kids had no choice but to sit through it whether they were interested. At the end of the assembly, the first person allowed to leave was Mrs Viper. Normality resumed as soon as she had disappeared back into her CEO's office for some essential education business behind locked doors.

"Miss, Miss, let me show you something." Mr Josiah said, walking next to me. He had his assembly notes and slush container under one arm while simultaneously trying to catch the attention of the young female science teacher walking close by. He produced his phone.

"What is it?" I pleaded stupidity whilst looking at a lengthy WhatsApp conversation.

"Miss, it's our humanities WhatsApp group. Look here, Mr Brand, commenting on the new OFSTED framework. Miss Smith is sharing this cool clip on source analysis. You should join. It is a great tool."

He had not given up, probably believing he could somehow engage me in this group. I looked at him sceptically.

"I see that Miss Smith shared this clip at quarter to midnight?! I am sorry; I do not wish to be in a group that contacts me after 5 pm. It's not healthy," I continued, walking towards my classroom, "the school has a duty of care towards staff. Like I proposed yesterday, if the school pays for my phone and the bills, I will look at those WhatsApp messages during personal preparation and planning times."

I walked off, suspecting that Mr Josiah tried so hard to promote this group because it was probably one of his performance management targets. He understandably wanted to achieve it.

Just as I arrived at my classroom, I spotted Ted and John passing by.

"Hey boys, thank you for saving the morning."

They walked over to me immediately, smiling.

"Eva, why does everyone lose their minds when Viper is in the building?" Ted asked, clearly amused.

"I know, right? It is unreal, but honestly, I am the same. She is scary," I said, "Imagine you had not been able to fix the screen. Mr Josiah would have had a meltdown."

"He did. Trust me."

"Guys come in quickly. I have biscuits."

"Oh, Eva, we can rely on you."

I unlocked my secret stash of goodies. For Ted and John, I always had biscuits or cake. In return, any IT problems I experienced were seen to and fixed immediately.

"John, are you off to a festival in half-term?"

"Yes, we are going to stay three nights in Denmark. Mary is going to perform. I will be there to support her. Hopefully, it won't rain. Last year was a washout."

"Wow, and Ted, will you join as well?" I asked cheekily.

"Ha, you know tent life is not for me."

"Same here. I considered glamping, but I have to admit if an event is not in a city with a hotel, I am not available."

"My son said a while back he suffered from OSA," said Ted.

"What is that?"

"Outdoor sleepover aversion," Ted said, adding," he self-diagnosed."

"Yes, I have that too."

John asked, "Guys, have you ever slept in a tent?"

"No. Why risk it?" John replied.

"Guys, I have. I was around eight and stayed at my friend Katja's datscha, and the parents said we could sleep in a tent in the garden," I said, "By midnight, I had snuck back into the datscha."

"Maybe Bella would like camping," John suggested.

"I doubt it. I think OSA is genetic. It runs in the family."

"See you later. Kids are coming. I need to educate the next generation."

"Thank you." They said in sync, holding up the biscuits like beer glasses.

THURSDAY, 9:10 AM

The group of little ones from year 7 was not as innocent as most outsiders would probably think. They had a fancy new subject that focused on learning how to learn, and they did not feel like learning anything, especially not how to learn. They were a problematic group. Teachers dreaded them. I liked most of the kids. They were ok on their own, in the playground or the canteen. As a group, however, they were almost unteachable. And yes, I knew my non-teacher friends, overlords, and parents disagreed with my assessment. However, most teachers who faced this group agreed. Whenever 7W was mentioned in the factory, eyes opened wide, experienced teachers wanted to pull their hair out, and teaching assistants had more than one story to tell.

I was lucky. I had the support of two teaching assistants with this group. Yet, it was still not enough, considering twelve out of 29 kids had special educational needs of varying levels. The kids' form tutor came along, too. It was not his job to do this, but he had a planning lesson and sacrificed it to support this lesson, hoping that the presence of the form tutor made a difference in group dynamics. I was thankful. It was four grown-ups to 29 kids, an excellent ratio on paper. In reality, it did not make a difference. Seventeen minutes later, despite warnings, names on the whiteboard for visual reminders, and the following of every step of the school's behaviour policy, there were still too many disruptions to justify starting the lesson.

Suddenly, thunder!

"Sit down."

There was this silence I and the other grown-ups, and probably many of the kids had been waiting for. This silence kept being disrupted by six hardcore individuals, all of them boys, who did not feel that the rules applied to them. Mr Sullivan appeared out of nowhere - his keys dangling beside his weak leg.

"I do not want to hear another word. Miss is waiting. Sir is waiting. Your teaching assistants are waiting," he shouted with military precision towards the six troublemakers, "Stop wasting everyone's time."

They obliged.

But why? Why was there no silence when four adults had been in the room already, equally as qualified, some more so than this overlord? I knew. From the primary factory onwards, those kids were taught about hierarchy. Slideshows after slideshows had drilled the factory's hierarchy in their little minds. At the top, of course, there was the CEO. She only had to look at a kid, and that kid would need a nappy even after having been toilet-trained ten years ago. Next came the high-vis crew, the team of overlords with walkie-talkies. They had the power to take kids out of class, to send kids off to another school for a day, to check a kid's phone without permission and to scream and shout at them. This layer of the feudal system had permission to go to a kid's house without being invited, to knock on doors when kids were ill, and to refuse to write college references. These people had the real power, and they exercised it. From a young age, the kids learned that those people's instructions needed to be followed because they had more power to punish than the regular serfs, who were mostly powerless. The ones who marked their books, showed up every day, tried not to raise their voice, sat till midnight to prepare lessons, printed worksheets in different languages, had snacks in the drawer for those kids who had not eaten all day, neglected their kids, had no family life. The serfs had to follow the behaviour policy. Most of those steps had no impact when hard-core offenders were involved.

"Get started with your gap-fill activity, please."

I used the silence to kick off the lesson. Nobody spoke; everyone got started. Mr Sullivan looked stern. The other four adults looked at each other from all corners, and we thought the same. The silence would not last long. Three minutes later, Mr Sullivan walked out, and within seconds, the noise level of a building site returned. The unteachables were unteachable. I felt sorry for the kids who came to the factory to learn, the ones who were inquisitive, the ones who almost looked scared amongst this noise, who looked at us four adults with hopeful eyes, begging for silence. Their parents had no money to send them to private factories and no time to homeschool them. They were stuck in what looked like an asylum of the unwilling. I taught them, and so did the teaching assistants and the form tutor. Two boys were removed by an overlord in high vis halfway through the lesson. They would be back the next lesson and act precisely the same way.

"Miss, I want to study politics and history for A level next year. Do you think I can make it? Will you be my teacher?" Chantelle, the noisy girl from the lunch queue, asked me when she arrived at my classroom.

"You can study history and politics. It is a great combination, and you have the skills for it. You write excellent essays, and you think critically," I said happily, "If you keep up to date with UK and US politics, you should be fine."

Chantelle grew two inches.

"As to whether I am teaching you, that is too early to tell. We teachers get our timetable at the end of the school year. The A-level lessons sometimes change, depending on how many kids there are."

"Oh, Miss, I want you to be my teacher."

"Do not pick a subject for the teacher. You need to want to study a subject. Teachers may leave halfway through your A level or get ill. If you want to know about a subject, you are much more likely to complete the course, no matter the teacher."

"Makes sense. You are probably right."

I took the register and wondered why Hoodie Boy had failed to arrive at my class. The usually hard-working girls were distracted.

"Sara, how is your source analysis going?"

Sara smiled and whispered, "Look, Miss, do you like the green or pink one more."

She pointed to two photos of prom dresses in some catalogue or bridal magazine.

"I like the green, but I would prefer it even more if you completed your history work and worried about prom once the exams are over."

"Sorry, Miss, but it will be too late by then. Everyone is getting their dresses now," Sara explained, "we also need to book hairstylists and makeup artists. They want to know what style we like so they can plan. Miss, this is a big mission. We cannot leave it to the last minute."

"But what exactly are you celebrating at prom when you fail your exams because you were preparing your hair and make-up rather than doing revision?" I wanted to know.

Sara looked at me, disappointed.

"Miss, you do not understand the urgency of the situation, but ok, I will do it during break time."

"Good."

They had neither sat nor passed a GCSE but planned to spend £500 on an evening celebrating the end of school. Spending money like that seemed odd to me. How did the kids have so much money when half were on free school meals, and why would parents give them this money?

"Guys, please make sure you use the criteria on the board to complete a self-assessment."

At that moment, the bell rang, and Sara got up to leave.

"Sara, please sit down and complete your self-assessment."

"But Miss, the bell went," Sara said with a whiney voice.

"Miss is the bell." The rest of the class said in unison. They knew. They had heard me say it before more than once. I walked row after row and checked each student's book. The last one I looked at was Sara's.

"You are dismissed." I smiled.

Proms had gotten out of hand over the last few years. The cars that arrived near the school on prom day were so big and long that they could only drive straight. Nobody could navigate any of those bus-length limousines through the side roads in town. On prom evening, it was best to hide at home. My factory's prom was usually held on the first Friday in July. Year 11 kids would be dropped off in their presidential cars to attend an assembly. The parents would come separately. After their last assembly, the kids would drive the short journey to the party, where some serfs and overlords would supervise their dinner and dance. Most parents did not know of the after-parties, which went unsupervised by school staff and required an additional, often more revealing outfit. They bought into the promises of their kids and the money-making scheme that was Prom.

THURSDAY, 11:20 AM

Anxiety, the self-appointed enforcer, which in equal measure kept me busy and disabled, had knocked on my classroom door. It was nearly my observation lesson. I locked myself into my room and spent all my break time inside. I wanted to avoid seeing anyone or being interrupted whilst going over the observation lesson for the last time. I had done it several times, but a lot depended on it. The pile of paperwork was ready. The books had been lined up on the front desk, ready for the kids to take to their desks when they entered. The PowerPoint displayed an engaging task. Learning objectives and keywords were on the board. I had included all the tick-box-worthy elements: numeracy, the promotion of British values, spiritual, moral, social and cultural development points, real-life links, pair work, writing frames, independent learning, literacy tasks, and, of course, my subject history, specifically the suffragettes. I had left out the peer assessment, which I knew would have made the lesson *outstanding* on paper. I planned to be good. That was my promise to myself. To be *good* only, not *outstanding*, because *outstanding* meant more work. I wanted to avoid any extra work at all costs. Once the overlords had judged anyone outstanding, this person had no break. They would suddenly act as mentors and coaches, lead professional development sessions, and show others how this teaching business was done for free. More community service. I wanted to teach, mark, prepare, go home, and have a life unrelated to education. I wanted no extra titles, no promotions and no freebie add-ons.

I greeted the kids by the door, smiling at each one to create a positive atmosphere. I felt like I could do this. My mood lifted, and the anxiety drained away. As soon as my observation lessons started, I always felt an enormous weight lift off my shoulders. I became an Oscar-worthy actress who would be on point. The Suffragettes was a great topic; it linked with the General Election that day. It was as if the universe had spoken to me. It gave me an excellent opportunity to connect to current affairs even though I was teaching a history lesson. Twenty minutes into the lesson, Mr Tracer, my observer, had yet to turn up.

Bang.

All of a sudden, the door burst open. Two

year 11 boys whom I did not teach ran in. They pushed aside desks that were in their way, got to the back row and grabbed Nadim by his collar. A zoo erupted, and all sorts of noises started: screaming, screeching and shouting, the sound of desks and chairs being pushed around on the hard floor. Nadim tried to free himself, but the two older boys wanted to drag him out of the classroom. Nadim was half pulled over a desk. I took two steps towards the bundle of boys when Mike, the on-site police officer, jumped in, grabbed the two-year-11 boys, and dragged them out of the room.

“Sorry, Miss." Mike apologised and disappeared.

What had just happened? Mike was always on-site, but he had never entered my classroom. He was this invisible ghost in the background. I had never seen him in action.

"Nadim, are you alright?"
"Yes, Miss," Nadim, fixing his tie, said, "I think they have beef with my brother."
"Are you okay with continuing, or would you like to leave?"
"Miss, all is good. I will stay."

I disagreed in my head. All was not good, but if Nadim, the victim, said all was good, I could not make him leave. The shock would set in later. The violent methods of the Suffragettes were discussed, and paragraphs were written. I walked past the kids, checking their work, suggesting improvements, correcting spelling mistakes and praising work done. I could not help thinking there had been police in every factory I had ever worked at, apart from the private factory. Private factories did not need police on site. Interesting. They may, however, have bodyguards for kids from high-net-worth families.

Out of character, my line manager did not turn up for the lesson, so I decided to include the peer assessment. I could be outstanding without anyone looking. I was glad when the lesson ended and reported the incident to the Head of Year and Nadim's form tutor. If those two year 11 boys felt bold enough to walk into a classroom in the middle of a lesson, who knew what they would do when no one was looking outside the factory gates?

It was unlike Mr Tracer not being at school and not turning up for an agreed observation, which now needed to be rescheduled. I would have to go through this process again, losing another night to anxiety. I had hoped this would be my last observation this academic year, having survived successfully the previous ones in October and January.

Ajinder and Cara were already eating.
"Come over."

I smiled and gestured that I would be coming. First, I had a look at the cover board. That is when I found out that Tracer was not in the factory. He had not forgotten my lesson, but he was off-site. Interesting. An overlord took a day off just before the upcoming spring half-term, which was the official deadline for handing in any resignations. That was a sign not of illness but probably a job interview with another factory. Leaving a factory required planning. An escape was only possible at Christmas, Easter and in the summer. The notice had to be handed in long before this. I wondered where Tracer might end up. There were plenty of secondary factories in the area, a few more in our academy trust, who constantly invented new positions and needed people because nobody wanted to stay. I took my lasagna from the fridge and got in line for the microwave.

"Have you voted yet?"

"Oh, is there an election? Is it today?" Lip-filler Drama, Josie asked in a stupid voice.

"Yes, guys, but the polling stations are open till ten tonight."

"Oh, I might go later, but really, they are all the same, aren't they?" Music, Hugh figured.

Drama Josie and Music Hugh should have been

a couple. They matched intellectually.

"Ah, but Love Island is on tonight; I don't think I can make it."

"Oh man, yes. I have to see this."

I felt helpless. People were lost in a vacuum of uncritical acceptance. They did not mind the status quo. They did not desire change, for they had fallen into political quarantine. Undoubtedly, teachers should want to vote. All was not well in the factories across the country. Change was needed. Cash was needed. Common sense was needed. Police on-site should not be required. Music and drama were the first subjects to go when the government made cuts to subjects, but lip fillers and Love Island were great distractions, so I stood there thinking this country deserved what it got. After ten minutes of standing around, tempted to repeat my suffragette lesson from earlier to the ignorant teachers who could not be bothered to vote, my lasagna was finally ready, and I sat next to Cara and Ajinder.

"Cara, I have not seen you since Monday's year team meeting. Where have you been hiding? Any more hairdresser incidents?"

Cara and I burst out laughing, remembering the session on Kofi's hairdressing skills, which went unappreciated by Sarah and Mrs Slump.

"Eva, I am exhausted. I have spent the last two days trying to find a work experience place for

Adil, you know who."

"Adil, of course, chucked a book and glue sticks at Joanna yesterday."

"Typical. This boy needs sorting."

"Yes, that is what I am trying to do. Get Adil out of here into the real world. But I doubt he would turn up for a placement."

"Poor Joanna, I felt sorry for her. She is not in today. I assume she went to her GP after all. I hope she also contacted the union. She was at a crisis point the other day. The overlords need to get their act together."

"What would you like to eat tomorrow night?"

"Ajinder, whatever you make for me. My belly loves your food."

I slapped my stomach a few times.

"Girls, I have to go. I can visit the town to see two potential work placements for our gangster boy."

THURSDAY, 1:25 PM

The playground was busy. Not many kids tried to hide inside the building as the sun lured them outside. I walked around the corner of my building, and by the door was Hoodie Boy with his head hanging and hands in his pockets.

"Hey Mikhail, how are you?" I said, thinking that one day I would call him Hoodie Boy by mistake and get in trouble.

"Hello, Miss, alright." He said quietly.

I unlocked the door.

"Do you want to come in?"

Without answering, he followed me inside, scrambled around in his pocket and took out some scrunched-up notes and a few coins.

"Thank you for paying for my shopping last night."

He handed me the money, looking sheepishly.

"No problem Mikhail."

"How is your mum?" I asked.

"She is ok. She had an operation on her knee, and it was pretty complicated, so she has not been home for several weeks," Mikhail said shyly, “she is always in and out of hospital. My dad is a lorry driver. He goes to Scotland a lot, so he is rarely home."

"Wow, that sounds like you have much to do at home."

"Yes, when my dad is away, I have to take my siblings to nursery and school in the mornings and sometimes pick them up in the afternoons. I look after them, give them food and all that stuff."

I was shocked to hear this. I had always imagined that Mikhail was just nasty, but it turned out that he had more to do than most kids or adults.

"You must be tired. Do you even have time to do any revision?"

"Not really. I will fail anyway."

Mikhail sounded as if he had already given up.

"Sorry for messing around in your lessons and missing your lesson this morning. I had a dentist appointment."

"Look, try to do your best in the upcoming exams. Here are some clips you can watch on YouTube," I took a pen and paper and started writing, "Let me also write down when each exam is taking place in history, and maybe you find the time to watch some of those clips beforehand."

I knew there was not much anyone could do at this point, especially with Mikhail's responsibilities at home. It was late in the year to put other interventions into place.

"If you ever feel like you just want to sit down alone or revise, you can come here apart from Tuesdays when I have lunch duty. You could also go to the learning support area. They have a study area away from everyone.

"Ok, Miss, thank you for the YouTube clips."

"No worries, good luck."

"Thank you."

Mikhail walked out of the room, and I sat down. I felt guilty for labelling Mikhail as a lesson disrupter, wishing he had gotten arrested on Monday and calling the overlords on him. I felt like a terrible teacher. How had the factory not realised that he had all these responsibilities? I emailed his form tutor and the learning mentor team. They could put in place some help, even though his time in the factory was nearly over. He probably needed better grades to stay here to complete his A-levels, but I had to try and help. The afternoon lessons went in a daze. Firstly, I felt drained, and secondly, I could not stop thinking about Mikhail's life. What if he had gotten arrested on Monday? Who would have picked up his siblings with his mum in the hospital and his dad driving lorries around this island? There did not seem to be much family support around either. Where was everyone? I tidied my room, grabbed more books to mark and set off towards the main building. It was a glorious day, and I would have loved to sit in a pub with a glass of white wine and do nothing.

THURSDAY, 4:05 PM

I saw the hall full of kids from the corner of my right eye. After-school detentions were invented for those souls who had not turned up for detention with their regular serf or committed a more serious crime, like causing a fire alarm on purpose or like Tango, who was caught smoking on the field, denying it with a cigarette in her hand. By the end of the year, every teacher had played the role of jailor. Most of the kids I saw were there in September, December and March. The punishment made no difference. Once a year, I had to bring my marking down into the hall and sit with the kids for an hour. An hour wasted on behalf of all of us. But not today.

"Mami, Mami, nothing happened. I did not get detention." Bella shouted over the fence.

"See, Baby Bella, that's what I said." I had my thumb up.

Bella came running towards me and gave me a big hug.

"Mami, sir said I can give him my literacy homework tomorrow, just like you told me."

"Fantastic. When we go home," I replied, "let's put the homework straight into your bag. Ok?"

"Yes."

We passed queues of people lining up to vote whilst driving towards our area.

"Bella, do you know who I went to see this morning?"

"No, who?"

"I went to see your headteacher, Mr Hammond, to ask whether he would allow you to go on holiday in a week. He said yes."

"Yippie." Bella threw her arms up in the air.

"And do you remember where we are going now?"

"Home," Bella shouted.

"Not yet, Bella. First, we go to the little church at the end of our road because Mami needs to vote."

"Yes, now I remember you must pick the boss people for the country."

"Yes, sort of like the boss people. The big boss person is the monarch, and we cannot vote for them. They are just there because they are born into a certain family," I explained, "but people vote for who they think would be good to represent them in Parliament. They will try to pick the person who would help them best to solve their problems. Like in school when you vote for a form rep."

"Will there be many people to pick from?"

"A few."

"But how do you know who is best?"

"Usually, each person is part of a team, and each team has different ideas on improving schools or hospitals. Most people listen to promises."

"But Mami, people can lie. Sometimes Abbu makes promises, and he does not keep them."

"Well, that is true. Maybe Abbu should not be a politician."

We both laughed.

"No, Abbu should not be a politician."

I thought that Bella's dad would make the perfect politician simply because he made a lot of promises which he did not keep. There was plenty of parking outside the church. The believers could not be restricted. We just left the car on the side of the road. Together, we walked into the little church. I said my name and there it was on the big register. A little old lady gave me my ballot paper. Nobody checked whether I was who I was. The lack of identity checks was a different approach to continental voting, where I had to bring my ID card. I could have been anyone or sent anyone.

I took Bella to one side and showed her the long paper.

"Look, here are all the names of the people.

Now I have to pick someone. Mami needs to go behind the curtain over there."

I pointed at the flimsy curtains that separated the polling booths from one another.

"Please wait here, Bella, one minute, ok?"

"Ok," Bella whispered.

I walked behind the curtains, pulling a funny face towards Bella. I made my cross next to my preferred boss. He was the one who wanted to invest in education. Then I folded the sheet, walked to the polling box, and waved Bella over. She came running to me. I gave her the ballot paper and told her to put it into the polling box.

"Wow, Bella, we're done. We have voted."

We got back in the car and were home three minutes later.

"Elizabeth, we have just voted for the next boss person."

Bella excitedly shouted across the road, and Elizabeth had to laugh.

"Bella, I have also voted for the next boss person," she replied, still laughing.

"I am going to see a friend in Manchester next week. Would you mind watering my plants?" she asked.

"No problem, just leave me the key over the weekend. See you later."

THURSDAY, 7 PM

After pizza dinner, Bella remembered her food technology creation that had caused us to do a midnight shop last night. I pretended to be full and distracted her by asking her to teach me the Bollywood dance moves she had learned at Azma's house the previous night. There was no rest for the wicked and beautiful.

"Mami, let's find the music on YouTube. I will show you how to dance."

It took us less than five minutes to find the correct song, and we spent the next hour dancing together. By the end of it, I was exhausted.

"Mami, you are a great dancer but need more energy."

"Thank you, baby Bella. It's good to see that you can keep going longer. Maybe you want to be a dancer when you are older. What do you think?"

"No, Mami, I will join the police force."

Having put Bella to bed, I returned to the kitchen for tea and some marking. By 10 pm, voting was over nationwide, and the first few predictions came in. I watched the news and was immediately disappointed. It looked as though the party stuffed with privately educated people would go on to win. Little could be changed when too many people spent time sleeping with the enemy or when many did not carry a badge of political allegiance. More years of misery were in the pipeline. I had to look into moving abroad more seriously.

FRIDAY, 6:15 AM

I had a rough night with little sleep. My throat was scratching, and my monkey brain had kept me awake. Medication was needed quickly. Ever since I had become a mum, I resorted to strong tablets as soon as anything felt funny. There was no time to be sick. Life had to go on. I contemplated calling in sick. But after a brief audience with myself, I decided against it. Calling in sick was too much work, and the overlords would probably classify it as an avoidable sickness. Tomorrow was the weekend. I could probably pull through, and I wanted to avoid setting cover work. My head was unprepared to type lesson tasks that non-subject specialists could deliver. I also wanted to keep the appearance of my classroom intact. If I took today off, my room would resemble a war zone, with displays ripped off the walls, exercise books mixed up, and resources disappeared or destroyed. This would add to my workload for next week.

The overlords would count the days of my

absence, and I did not want trouble with them either. The type of trouble Science Mario encountered a few months ago. When he had broken his leg, he got several emails from overlords who had suggested he take a taxi to work each morning and evening at the cost of over £70 per day, despite being signed off by his doctor. With their medical degrees obtained at Wannabee University, the overlords knew better than any doctor and figured that Mario could teach sat down. He went along with his doctor's line, and with this self-induced character assassination in the eyes of the overlords, he had destroyed all future chances of promotion.

With a quick shower, a layer of makeup and two aspirins, I felt like I was no longer disintegrating. Bella took longer than normal, and while waiting, I tried not to stick my head right into my coffee mug. "Mother's Little Helper" from the Rolling Stones was shot out of the radio, and I thought this song could easily be adapted for teachers.

"Mama, I cannot find my PE kit."

"Have you looked in your wardrobe or next to the shoe rack?"

I wondered whether these were standard conversations in all houses with young kids.

"Hurry up, Bella, it's Friday, and traffic is always worse on a Friday, we need to have breakfast and leave soon."

"But Mami, I still haven't found my PE kit."

Bella zoomed towards me with her shoulders up and arms stretched out.

"Bella, when was the last time you had PE?"

"On Tuesday."

"I will go and check in the boot whilst you have breakfast."

"I also need one pound, please?"

"Yes, I will give it to you when we arrive at the breakfast club. For now, I will find the PE bag."

Twenty minutes later, we and the PE kit were in Friday traffic with people behaving like they had bought their driving licence in the local corner shop.

"Baby, story time."

"I am ready, Mami."

"So, imagine when Mami was small and we forgot our PE kit, we had to do PE in our underwear."

Bella burst out laughing

"No, you didn't."

"Yes, no joke, baby. This is why I always had my PE kit," I hinted with a serious face, "teachers did not care if anyone felt embarrassed. We had just to join in."

"Mami, that's not nice. I wouldn't want to do that." Bella said, looking out the window, bopping her head to the music.

Bella wore civilian clothing, jeans, sneakers, a pink shirt with a glitter heart and a blue cardigan. I handed over the mandatory £1 donation for Bella to be allowed to look like an average kid or a kid who went to school in continental Europe.

"Bella, who are you collecting money for today?"

"For the box babies go into when they are born early."

"Ah, incubators."

Bella nodded.

"Yes, Mami, the hospital has no money. The school will send the money."

"That's good," I said.

However, I felt this was the government's responsibility. A rich nation like this one that kept celebrating itself as the *world-beating* this and that and who had plundered so many other nations should be able to provide hospitals with incubators for little newborns. But here we were. Kids ran in circles, paid for non-uniform days, and sold cakes in a country ranking among the top ten economies. The kids made sure babies would not die. Society clapped for those kids. Yes, it was admirable. But why didn't anyone teach the kids to hold the government to account? Why not demand taxes be spent on incubators rather than weapons, war, non-existent bridges, or plane decorations? Donations and fundraisers were almost second nature to many people. Money was handed out without questioning why society had to donate when people had already paid taxes. And how come this was celebrated as a success when surely it was a sign of government failure? I drove off thinking about how big businesses avoided paying taxes, got a discount or conveniently negotiated their tax rate. All while people were caught up in this mental prison of fundraising, not realising they were short-changed.

FRIDAY, 8:35 AM

I parked the car at the factory, took my bags to my room, dropped them on the desk, and returned to the main gate. From the distance, I could already see that Mr. Josiah was overexcited and hyped up.

"Miss, you are not looking too well."

"Thanks. I feel really ill. Didn't sleep too well either. You seem cheerful."

"Miss, get yourself a fresh juice after school and have an early night. You should also consider cold showers in the morning." Doctor Josiah suggested.

I grunted, hiding my disagreement. The one thing I needed in the morning was hot coffee, not a cold shower. That was for masochists. I did not want to be by the gate this morning, especially not with noisy pretend doctor Mr Josiah, but I had to stand here because I was part of the factory's greeting committee.

"Good morning...good morning ...good morning..."

Mr Josiah and I kept repeating the mantra. The

greeting committee claimed more territory than the immediate area outside the factory's gate. Some factories extended theirs all the way to the nearest train station.

We smiled, I with dead eyes and Mr Josiah with zig-zag animated cartoon eyes. The snake of impatient kids that had formed outside the school gates was delayed because of the additional uniform check. Anyone contaminated with individualism had to be caught out before entering the factory grounds. Access denied! This was where the surveillance society started, and it would never end. Mr Josiah and I, the bouncers of the day, were the ones who had the power to let someone in or send them home or wherever else they may choose to go. Some of the top private schools in the country did not impose school uniforms on kids, yet they regularly sent kids to Cambridge and Oxford.

"Good morning, Miss."

Hanad, one of my students, was there. He was on doughnut duty, and I handed him some cash. He went to the supermarket around the corner to buy the customary Friday doughnuts for our form time.

Mr Josiah pulled up the left sleeve of his black banker suit jacket.

"Miss, look at my new watch."

It was dark blue and looked bigger than those

Fitbits that had been in vogue a few years ago and which I had never bought into.

"What does it do?"

"This counts steps, calories, and water intake in addition to telling the time." Mr Josiah explained excitedly.

"How did humanity survive up to this point without this gadget?" Cynical sarcasm.

"Miss, really, why are you always so sceptical? You should try one of those."

"In the olden days, people ate when they were hungry, drank when thirsty, slept when they were tired. Why do you want to assess everything in terms of efficiency?"

"It's not assessing. It's just keeping track, seeing that you are doing the right thing for your body."

"I don't want any gadgets in my life, Sir. I do not wish to improve," I replied," Don’t you feel more pressure and stress because you have to meet specific targets?"

"Stress is good. It makes us work harder. Be our best self," Mr Josiah explained, "I am sure one day you will change your mind Miss."

I was sure I would not change my mind. I noticed that many people were using apps and gadgets all day. People were always busy trying to improve, but for what? A pot of oats with super-berries gobbled down whilst walking, almost running to the train station. Women in trainers on their feet and heels in the office ran up escalators hoping to burn three calories. Work emails typed on public transport. The tourist was pushed out of the way under the train. Special cycle outfits are worn to achieve a personal best before even arriving at work. Everything was optimised. No breath wasted on life. No app for living, no app for fun.

"You see, I am trying to live like my grandparents. They had never scheduled running sessions, counted steps, or learned anything after work. They came home, ate whatever they wanted, and were still not fat. They drank alcohol, had parties with friends and lived way into their 80s."

With one eye, I looked over to the left. I saw more and more kids accumulating, usually an accurate predictor of trouble to come, just like having a quiet toddler in the room next door. It tended to spell disaster.

"But, Miss, times have changed."

"They sure have."

And there it was, the commotion I had been waiting for.

“Fight, fight, fight.”

The screaming and the dreaded chants were there for all to hear. App man and I ran towards the circle that had formed. Sana and Simran were pulling each other's hair, cursing and being egged on by the crowd that looked like it was taking bets but not sides. Some probably filmed this spectacle ready to be shared later on some social media outlet. I pushed past the ring of spectators, as did Mr Josiah, but it was not easy. There were too many of them. No serf ever wanted to push too hard or appear too aggressive. That could lead to an investigation and endless justifications in front of overlords, parents or worse, lawyers. The kids moved a bit more for me. For Mr Josiah, they made it a bit more complicated. By the time he made it close to the wrestling match, I had already gotten hold of Sana's arm.

"Stop!"

I tried my best teacher's stare into Sana's angry eyes, and it worked. Her face resembled that of a fighter ready to punch. I had been in this situation before when I was a teaching assistant, and a year 8 boy had held a big hole puncher over my head, threatening me. Sana's stare of anger was cold. There was not much anyone could do unless they had been trained in one-to-one combat, but that was not offered in continuous professional development sessions. Not yet. I would have taken up the offer. Sana realised that she could not escape this situation and that anything else would result in more drama for her. Her facial features softened into sadness, and tears appeared in her eyes. Her ferocious stare turned blank, and some overlord pulled Sana away into the distance. Mr Josiah made it through to Simran and moved her away from the scene towards me. With Mike's help, the crowds started to disperse. Nothing to see anymore. The Friday morning show was over.

"Move inside. Go inside."

Some overlords appeared from the factory. Forgotten was the all-important uniform check; green, instead of white socks, secretly entered the building.

I saw Mr Josiah looking flustered as if he had lost something. Maybe he got hurt trying to get to Simran. It can happen when kids form crowds. I had no time to ask him, but I was sure he would be okay. I was tasked to take Simran to the internal exclusion zone, the place for the worst offenders. The overlords, the Head of Year, and learning mentors would deal with her later. This time, they might give a punishment exceeding a twenty-minute cooldown. Chantelle, the reformed gangster girl, suddenly appeared next to us.

"Miss, do you know whose watch this is?"

She dangled Mr Josiah's broken watch in front of my nose. His life monitor must have come loose, fallen off his wrist and been stepped on. It did not look like it would count anything anymore. Over there, he was alive yet looking very concerned.

"That's Mr Josiah's watch." I nodded in his direction.

"OK, Miss, thank you."

Chantalle walked over to Mr Josiah, who was still scanning the floor. She handed him the watch. I did not see how Mr Josiah reacted, but I imagined it was not a happy emotion. Maybe something good would come of it. By the end of the day, he might realise that he was still breathing even though he had no reminder whether his vital stats were in line with survival needs. There were no reminders, trackers or counters of calorie intake, water, or steps, and he would still be walking around. It would be a miracle. It would almost be like walking on water.

Sana and Simran remained in banishment most of the day, where they sat on chairs that had been screwed to the floor because kids had been known to throw them around, bang their heads against the wall and run in circles screaming. They were provided with work but did very little, supervised by mentors who would have to try to avoid further fighting. They were allowed to jump the queue at lunchtime because they had to have as little contact with their peers as possible. Neither were downcast or happy about it. They had become indifferent.

At the end of the day, they had to be picked up by their parents at different times, probably before everyone else was about to leave. And on Monday, they would start again. This circle of factory life would go on and on. The same things would be done without any change, but different outcomes would be expected. It was an insane kamikaze mission.

I walked to my classroom, changing the lyrics from "Friday I am in love" to "Friday I am in a fight".

"Good morning, beauties," I said to my form group.

The girls loved it, the boys pretended to hate it, but they smiled anyway. Doughnut duty Hanad pulled the change from his school uniform shirt pocket and handed out the doughnuts whilst I took the register. This was our Friday morning routine.

"Yes, Miss."
"Here, Miss."
"Yeah."
"Hm."

From their responses, I determined when each kid had gone to bed last night or this morning. Today, I had important work to do. Each tutor had been tasked with asking for every child's nationality, noting it and returning the information to the main office. This did not sit well with me. I asked myself why the school needed this information and why parents had yet to be asked directly to provide it. It was an odd thing to ask of serfs. I decided to forget it. Instead, I walked around my room, discussing plans for the weekend, the future, and life. Friday's registration time was a time to be human.

I sometimes considered myself a maverick. Described in the dictionary as an *unorthodox or independent-minded person*. The teachers I loved from my school days were the ones who broke the rules when it made teaching more fun. It took bravery to dissent, to be original and rebellious, but it was worth it. Everyone was busy flying through their life in a fighter jet. I wanted to swap the fighter jet for a kite. Go up and down and enjoy the wind. Fly off script. Bend rules. The mavericks were always happier. Released from the prison of monotony, we lived in the here and now. Overlords despised us, for it was the mavericks that could demand attention from a crowd and organise a union. The factory made room for too many living corpses with worried eyes and skeletons haunted by the ghosts of expectations. Whenever I noticed another maverick teacher, my heart jumped. We were mad, adventurous, eccentric, radical, courageous, and kind to ourselves. We were the out-group. What was not to love? The maverick held up the mirror to society and the factory. And in it, the conformists could see what they did not dare to be. Therefore, they hated and admired the maverick in equal measure. Of course, I understood that conformity also meant safe income, a paid mortgage and dinner on the table, but maybe if more serfs were a little more maverick, everyone would benefit.

I told all my groups I was not feeling very well, and they responded by being a little less noisy. The A-level kids worked away on their exam preparation, completing questions with the help of the mark scheme and my input. The little ones created storyboards about the Crusades. This was a good morning, and I could rest a bit before my break time playground duty. I was bursting after being unable to go to the toilet since 8 am before greeting committee duty. No wonder teachers were suffering from urinary tract infections all the time.

FRIDAY, 11:15 AM

"I have noticed you have not yet returned the nationality paperwork." Mrs Slump said, washing her hands.

"Yes, that's right," I replied, "I do not feel comfortable creating a register of nationalities. If the school wants such a register, they can write to the parents and get this information."

Mrs Slump seemed flustered and struggled for words.

"Well, the school wants us to do it. Would you mind if I came to your registration on Monday and did it?"

"Fine. I am on a trip on Monday so I won't be in form time anyway."

At least I did not have to take part in this spy activity. I arrived at my playground duty five minutes late, promptly to be told off by Mrs Winter, who was out again. Not only had I been late, but I had also forgotten my high-vis vest and was not talking to any kids. I needed this telling off.

"Sorry, I am on my period. I had to urgently go

to the toilet as I have a full teaching day."

That shut up, Mrs Winter.

"Oh, that's fine, but please engage with the students. They really enjoy it when we talk to them."

The teenage whisperer insisted on engagement. Engage with the kids in a secondary factory? During break time? Why? Which kid wanted to talk to a serf during break time? This could potentially spell social suicide for the kid. I walked towards the younger ones to engage in conversation about the weather. They spoke shyly and smiled, and so did I. We parted ways, happily avoiding each other ever after. Mrs Winter needed a reality check. Teens were trying to get away from grown-ups.

I walked slowly to my classroom after Mrs Winter rang the bell like a cow in the fields. This next lesson was meant to be a learning walk, a whistle-stop tour of seeing serfs at work. The overlords conducted those regularly and told teachers what the focus would be because they were such kind humans. As Mrs Viper announced earlier, this learning walk focused on numeracy. All teachers were teachers of numeracy! When Mr Sullivan and Mr Tracer, my line manager who had not turned up for yesterday's observation, appeared with clipboards in my A-level politics lesson, I stopped the kids from what they were doing.

"Oliver, can you quickly remind me of the proportional representation system?"

Oliver was confused as he had just been writing about the first-past-the-post system. However, this did not matter. We needed numeracy soundbites, anything related to numbers, percentages or equations. It took him two seconds to compose himself.

"The proportional representation system is an electoral system in which the distribution of seats corresponds closely with the proportion of the total votes cast for each party. For example, if a party gained 20% of the total votes, a perfectly proportional system would allow them to gain 20% of the seats."

"Thank you, Oliver, for this reminder. Please continue your essays."

I looked at the two overlords who ticked something on their clipboard, smiled their usual icey smiles and walked out. I, too, grinned a faux neutral smile and bore it. Mission accomplished. The overlords had been outmanoeuvred. This was a game serfs had to play. The longer we had been in the circus, the better we knew how to entertain the overlords and their alternate reality in return for a dead smile.

As was to be expected, plenty of emails needed binning in virtual space or ignoring because they were irrelevant to improving my teaching or my students' learning. I spent my lunch sorting through my inbox. An email stating that it was payday. Irrelevant. My bank account would momentarily notice before returning into the red. An email telling me that a new person had been employed in Finance. Irrelevant. An email to remind people to take part in the staff social. Irrelevant. But there was an email, *Book Look Feedback.* Now, that was interesting. I opened the attachment, and a vast self-congratulatory grin formed on my tired face. My plan had worked. There it was in black and white; *marking was frequent and effective, students engaged with the marking process, literacy was addressed through marking followed by self-assessment, and peer assessment was used and monitored by the teacher.*

This email was evidence of two things. Firstly, I knew how to mark and did it according to the policy. Secondly, and more importantly, overlords were fooled by the techniques serfs had to employ to please them. Had I left Hoodie Boy's book and those of his crew in the marking pile, my feedback would have looked different because three students had decided not to do what they were meant to do. I had done my job well. Yet, the decisions made by 16-year-olds could have seriously impacted how the overlords perceived my teaching ability. If I could not save the kid who did not want to learn, at least I had to save my ability to pay my bills.

FRIDAY, 1:45 PM

I had agreed to teach a sex and relationship education lesson after lunch. Although this was a compulsory subject, parents still had the right to withdraw their kids from the sex, if not the relationship part. Every year, the group got smaller as soon as relationship education was over and sex entered the curriculum. Sex made the factory population shrink, unlike in the real world. There were those parents who probably felt they could teach the topic better and others who simply did not want their kids to learn anything sex-related. The kids who were removed on request had to spend their lessons in the library and read. However, as soon as the lesson was over, their mates and friends would run to them and tell them in great detail what they had learned.

This group was a rowdy bunch, 19 boys and seven girls. Not great for this lesson, but they only had to spend the first two of a series of six lessons together, after which they would be separated along the lines of owners of male or female bodies.

"Miss, can we have practical sex education?" Rohail asked, smiling the biggest smile.

"No, Rohail, we cannot have practical sex education, but we can invite your dad to sit with you over the next few lessons to make sure you do not interrupt me again. How does that sound?"

"Woooooooooo."

The classroom erupted. Three minutes later, everyone had calmed down. The lesson continued. The attention-seeker did not speak for the rest of sex and relationship education, neither to me nor his friends. Many kids had misconceptions about what sex and relationship education actually looked like, and so did some parents. This may have been a reason why they removed their kids. In secondary factories, it covered topics such as consent, sexual exploitation, online abuse, grooming, coercion, harassment, rape, domestic abuse, forced marriage, honour-based violence and FGM. Kids learned the law about sex, sexuality, sexual health and gender identity. They looked at positive choices for themselves and at mental health. Really nothing too scary or even inappropriate, but this message was often lost, and some kids, such as Rohail, and some parents, thought sex ed would descend into porn viewing sessions. This was, of course, not the case. Porn was apparently already on the curriculum in ICT, at least in my form group. Some kids, mainly boys, tried to intimidate female serfs by making comments such as Rohail's. They had not banked on serfs, who were not easily intimidated or embarrassed by teenage boy talk.

Crash.

Bang.

The door flew open, and Giulio entered. He had kicked it as if this was the conventional way to enter late.

"Good morning, Giulio, thank you for joining us."

I handed him a worksheet. He scrunched it up and kicked it with his right foot nearly into the bin. Despite being impressed by his skills, I had to look professional.

"Stupid school, stupid class."

I remained calm and listened just like the rest of the class, who had stopped their task and watched this free movie.

"They say I have anger management problems," Giulio said and walked out again.

I did not comment but, in my head, uttered *no way.*

Mitch from across the room was worried about Guilio's safety.

"Miss, won't you go after him and make him come back?"

"No, he knows where we are, he can come here. We have work to do. I don't have time to run after one student who chooses to leave the classroom."

Running after Guilio would have set off a domino effect of anger management issues. I neither had the energy nor the interest in this. Instead, I emailed the learning mentors and the overlord in charge to let them know Guilio was running free and wild on the factory premises. I was amused and shocked at how some youngsters could verbally articulate their problems these days but felt unable to implement any changes. What if adults walked into their place of work proclaiming they had anger management problems? Nobody would care. If we did not manage our anger, we would find ourselves jobless quickly. However, the factories denied this reality.

"Miss, what if the door hit you? Or, what if a pupil hit you? Has anyone ever hit you in school?"

Mitch was highly inquisitive today.

"I would take my phone and call the police right into this classroom and ask them to start criminal proceedings. I would do the same as if I were hit in the street. I would call the police. School is not a law-free zone."

This sounded good, shut Mitch up, but it would probably never happen. The part on criminal proceedings that would never happen because overlords would try to hide any incident. It was also debatable as to a factory not being a law-free zone. Little gangsters would get away with more than in real life outside the gates. The age of criminal responsibility, one of the lowest in Europe, was mentioned in Citizenship lessons but ignored by the people in power. Inspectors marked factories down for exclusions, so we would all pretend to exist in a Buddhist monastery. Secretly, I had considered positioning myself close enough to one of the doors a few times. It really was just a matter of time before my head would split open and I could occupy the hospital for a few days. Paid vacation. Afterwards, I could claim compensation and retire to Sicily with a Harry Potter scar on my forehead. Sicily, that magnificent Mediterranean island. They even sold houses for one Euro in Sicily. I had this romantic idea of a little house without carpets made from stone in a tiny village in the middle of nowhere with Mount Etna sizzling behind me and great food and wine on the table under the blue sky in the sun.

FRIDAY, 2:50 PM

At least at the end of the day, I had no anger to manage. It was the last of my three planning, preparation and assessment lessons I had every week. The empty, quiet classroom induced nostalgia in me. It reminded me of my old school and my time with Anja, who lived in the school. As a kid, I imagined this was the coolest place to live, followed by living inside a supermarket or shopping centre where I could walk around all night and take whatever I wanted. Back then, I had yet to hear of Sicily. Kids still had to go to school on Saturday mornings, and some went to the nursery because many grown-ups had to go to work. Sometimes, my mama took me to work rather than sending me to the nursery or leaving me home when my papa was off work. Those were the days of fewer health and safety restrictions. I loved being there. Everything about it, the rooms, the chalk, the smell, the bell, the milling around. It was exhilarating.

My mum told me to sit next to some tall, lanky boy who would smile because he knew that for this lesson, he did not have to care so much about physics or mathematics, but he had the job of admiring my drawings. Sometimes, I sat in the little office next to the classroom, but mostly, I played with my best friend. Blonde Anja's dad was the caretaker in the school, and with this job came the flat inside the building on the ground floor. To get there, one had to go through the main entrance. There was no other entry or exit point. Even when it was dark, the weekend or the holidays, one always had to open the heavy grey doors of the school, turn left and walk down a huge corridor towards the music room. Opposite the toilets, there was Anja's flat. Having passed through a glass door where only the family had a key, one entered a squared area almost like a corridor from which we stepped into Anja’s flat. Anyone taken into the flat blindfolded would never have known they were inside a school. The flat looked like any other flat I had known.

Sometimes, on a Sunday, Anja and I quietly took the huge set of keys which belonged to Anja's dad whilst he was asleep. We had to remove this jailor's key from the hook next to the mirror in the hallway without creating noise. It helped that Anja's dad always had his afternoon nap on the sofa in the living room with the door slightly ajar and that he was a big snorer. We had to quietly sneak out of the flat and upstairs on tiptoes and in socks, where we would open a room and play school, write on the blackboard and read books. We felt like rogue soldiers on a mission not authorised by the generals. Our mission, however, lasted only a short time because Anja's dad only snored for around an hour or so after lunch. The keys had to be back on the hook before he woke up. Childhood was better in the times before mobile phones and CCTV.

On Saturdays, when I had come to school with my mama, Anja and I were often found in the playground climbing, jumping and finding imaginary treasures in the sand. But when the bell went, and hundreds of kids between six and 16 stormed out of the building for their break time, we ran inside the flat as fast as we could. Anja had a key to the flat, just like I had a key to mine. Even at five or six, this was normal in a country where most parents worked full-time. I was scared the first time we experienced this platoon of kids invading the playground. Those kids were all older and bigger. We rushed to Anja's dad's office next to the entrance, where blue-white smoke appeared under the door. When we opened the door to talk to Anja's dad, we heard him but did not see him. Teachers met here to smoke. Some stood outside the school building on the steps where they smoked with older students. Those weekends spent at school influenced my future career choice long before

I started school. For me, school symbolised finding things out. Being a teacher was my dream job.

I snapped out of my sentimental mood, opening emails sent by Lucy and Jo. Their completed essays on the Supreme Court were not perfect but much improved versions. Suddenly, the door opened.

"Sorry to bother you, but I have a few questions I forgot to ask you in our meeting the other day."

"How can I help you, Sam?"

"We got this email about volunteering on a Saturday to go to Thorpe Park. I said I would do it because it meets one of my standards," Sam said, "have you ever been away on a trip on a Saturday?"

"No. Honestly, I am too lazy for Saturday, weekend or residential trips, and because I have Bella, people do not bother asking me. Do you like theme parks?”

"Yes, always have done. Do you think we will be back on time?"

"You see, the other people want to get home too. Also, the kids that go along are usually the well-behaved ones. The trips are reward trips for attendance, achievement or whatever else the overlords can think of. So the kids that go tend to be back at the coach on time."

"And I really do not need to do this risk

assessment?

"No worries, this will have been done by whoever organised the trip."

"Good. I think I might do it to tick this trip box on the standards sheet."

"Yes. It is a good idea, especially if you like theme parks and rides."

"I am off to the Black Country Museum on Monday, so I won't see you till Tuesday. If you have any problems, please see Ajinder."

"Ah, one more question." Sam said, "Do you have any tips on reports? They are due soon as well."

"I usually write three standard sets of reports for girls - top kid, average kid, underachiever, then I change pronouns for any other version," I explained, "then I add in three things we are working on or will work on in the coming weeks."

"Could you show me an example, please? Not now, but maybe next week?"

"I can do better," I said, "I will email you my sets now, and then you can adjust them as you please."

"Wow, that would be amazing," Sam said.

I enjoyed mentoring Sam and tried to support her whenever possible. The report templates would save her a lot of time. Time was finite, and the inspectors and overlords had forgotten this due to lack of actual work. Just before Sam shut the door, I remembered the data entry.

"Sam, do not forget the data entry is also due."

"Done it."

"That's my girl. Top teacher."

Sam walked out, and all this trip talk reminded me to see Mr Josiah before going home.

At least three times a year and, in some places, up to six times, serfs entered all sorts of data about their little darlings into the humongous factory database. Kids became digits on a spreadsheet. I had to ensure I gave each kid a current working level and set three new targets. I had to analyse which free school meal kid was not doing so well, which newly arrived kid was making rapid progress, and which ethnic group was under or overperforming. Colour-coded spreadsheets were created by the Assistant Headteacher for Curriculum and Assessment and shared and discussed.

In some factories, kids's photos were placed in an office with coloured stickers to emphasise their failures or successes visually. Kids were dragged into these offices to see where they ranked in the bigger scheme. Some returned happy; others were crushed, and many were embarrassed by their photo as much as their position within their year group. At times, I felt like an accountant surrounded by numbers and graphs. But those numbers and graphs had human beings hidden behind them. A kid whose dog had died on the morning of an exam, another kid whose father might have walked out on the family the night before a mock or a kid whose grandma had just been diagnosed with a terminal disease. Often, it felt that none of this mattered. All was fine as long as the data looked according to plan, on track, on target, and the correct path. If there were a deviation off the track, there would be questions. Questions about the serf's teaching style, differentiation, planning, marking or behaviour management. Although life had ups and downs, stock markets had ups and downs, and nothing anywhere in the circle of life was forever just going up, downs were not allowed in factories. The only way was up.

Because of my trip on Monday, I only had three teaching days, as next Friday was INSET day. Friends and parents were confused about INSET day. According to the powers to be, it was *In-service Education and Training* Day, which children did not attend, and staff received training or were given time to complete administrative tasks. It was basically teachers taking on their kids' role on a non-uniform day. It was a day on which we tried not to die of boredom. Top-set teachers would be licking their way upward or wanting to climb the career ladder quickly. They were to be found in the hall sitting close to the overlords, forever nodding and making pointless contributions that prolonged any meeting. Success by proximity. In the middle of the hall were the dedicated, good teachers. The type of teachers who bought equipment out of their pocket. They came to school in the last two weeks of the summer holidays to decorate their rooms, wrote each child a birthday card, and were pretty much stand-by parents. In the back sat the mavericks who played bullshit bingo whilst the overlords did whatever they did. They were also well-liked by the kids because they had interesting stories to tell, made lessons engaging, and filled the air with a bit of rebellion against the system. They did get their kids to achieve top grades.

Most INSET days were boring but less formal than a regular work day. They centred on re-programming serfs with policies or initiatives. The overlords had the regrettable tendency to outsource the day. Consultants came in to tell a group of serfs how to teach their subject even though they already knew how it worked as they always did it. But this did not matter because these spiritual advisers earned at least £500 daily. If any serf were to fail an observation, the overlords could point to this session and say that they should have paid better attention and implemented the strategies suggested. Unmentioned was the fact that some consultants had not taught for ten years and were previously employed in a private school setting. They would probably run out of the average factory room crying and pulling their hair out less than five minutes into any lesson. Serfs endured this alienating infantilisation as part of their profession. They pretended to listen. Time for preparation and marking, or admin as per definition, was not really scheduled into INSET days but would have helped many of us tremendously. Just like the kids, we had to be entertained at all times. The whole day had to be planned through.

The worst INSET session I had ever participated in was on team building, where we had to throw balls at each other, find adjectives with the first letter of our name, and engage in little activities to make us work better as part of a team. This included a lot of eye-rolling, clock watching and near dissent. What utter rubbish! We had to endure these playground activities whilst, in the back of our minds, we were planning lessons.

However, there was something positive about some INSET days. We sometimes got to leave on time or even a little bit earlier. This meant I got to pick up Bella from school on INSET day. It was fun to see Bella jump out of the classroom. I only sometimes had this experience. On one INSET day a few years ago, I nearly missed it because I was chatting to a former student, Jeremy. We stood outside the classroom I believed Bella was educated in, only to be informed by Jeremy that year 2 was three doors down. I pretended to know this but did not since I never dropped Bella at the factory. My territory was the breakfast club in the nursery opposite, not the school. A secret WhatsApp group probably discussed my failure to find my child's classroom.

FRIDAY, 5:30 PM

I walked to the other building, but Mr Josiah was not in his room. As it was pretty late for a Friday, I thought he might have left until I heard suspicious noises from the Humanities office. Was Mr Josiah having a run in the office? Was he checking whether his broken watch with the health apps was picking up his steps? I walked towards the office door, and the heavy breathing had stopped, the door opened just as I wanted to grab the handle and out walked Gemma, the quiet wallflower from the finance department. Her face appeared to be flushed, perhaps a sign of deviant behaviour. Her hair seemed slightly out of place, but it was Friday afternoon. Had this been a case of a duel of saliva, or was it even more? I wanted to ask but stopped myself.

Mr Josiah was in the back of the office looking sheepish.

"Miss, how can I help you?"

"I was wondering whether there was anything we needed to do before Monday."

"Monday, why?"

He was clearly not back in thinking mode yet.

"The trip on Monday. Black Country Museum."

I reminded him with a smile.

"Ah, the trip. No. All is good. I have it sorted. We are all set. I must go now, Miss. Sorry, I'm running late; it's my mother-in-law's birthday dinner."

He walked out of the office.

"Well, have a great family night."

I could not resist making this comment.

Mr Josiah locked the office where he just had a practical sex education lesson with Gemma and walked off into the distance. Buildings helped to define character. There was a case for open plan offices to bring in line the disorderly elements who breached moral integrity.

Bella was bouncing on the mini-trampoline when I arrived. Her two pigtails jumped up and down beside her ears, a big grin on her face. When she spotted me, she took a massive jump off the trampoline and jumped right at me. We nearly fell from the force.

"Mami, are we going to Ajinder? Can I watch cartoons?"

"That's the plan, baby, but first we go home, leave our bags and get changed."

The traffic was similar to this morning. We listened to music and sang without really knowing any of the lyrics. It did not matter. We made them up and sang all the louder for it. Outside the house, the candle business lady from the opposite side of the street opened the door to the dog walker. The young man handed over the cute fluffy thing. Without a smile, she shut the door, having taken the dog. She meant business. Another transaction, just like having a cleaner or tutor. I had seen the dog walker often, on holidays, I had noticed him most days and always wondered why nobody in their house managed to walk this dog. It seemed very odd to have a dog, be at home all day and not find the time to walk the dog but instead pay someone to do it.

On a Friday night, I brought exercise books home, too. Not just one set, like on a regular night. It had to be two sets. There were two full days before I had to return to the factory. If I slacked over the weekend, I would be too far behind. Bella tried to lift and carry one of the bags inside, but it was impossible. She giggled and laughed.

"Mami, I need more food before I can carry this inside."

"Yes, that's why we will go to Ajinder in 20 minutes. Go get changed."

I put the kettle on and changed into civilian clothing. There was always time for a quick cup of tea. The good thing with Ajinder was that you could turn up at her house in whatever clothes.

It was so relaxing. I almost wanted to sleep there. I quickly checked around our small flat to see whether there was any washing lying around, put on a quick wash so that it would be ready to be hung up when we returned and sat down to go through this week's post.

I had gotten into the habit of collecting my letters throughout the week and dealing with everything on Friday evenings or Saturday mornings. There was the bill from the electricity and gas people, but I had a standing order, so it did not matter. Two companies tried to sell me home insurance, which was due soon, and there were three postcrossing postcards. They were the highlight of this little letter pile. The first card from Malaysia had a stunning photo of the Putra Mosque on it, and Annie, the girl who had written it, loved travelling. The stamps were unusual, too. The second card was much bigger than the average postcard, nearly twice the size, and it showed James Dean in the penny arcade. Michelle from California had sent it, and it had taken three weeks to travel. The third card, my favourite for this week, was the Charles Bridge in Prague. It was a black and white picture, probably taken in autumn or winter because it looked very dark, a little bit like the black and white crime movies I used to watch when she was around ten or eleven. When Bella came into the kitchen, she shuffled onto my lap.

"Are these the postcards for this week?"

"Yes, have a look. Which one is your favourite?"

Bella slowly looked at each one; she inspected not only the postcards but also the stamps.

"This one here," she held up the Malaysian mosque, "is the best postcard because it looks so pretty and sunny."

"My favourite one is this one," I said, "I walked across this bridge when I was around your age. I have been to Prague many times."

"Really, Mami, you walked on this bridge? Can we go there?"

"Yes, one day we can go there, but for now, we are off to Ajinder's."

"Can we hang them up?"

"We do that on Sunday when you are back from Abbu's. First, I need to go online and register the postcards on the website and thank the people who wrote them. We will hang them up once I have done that."

Next to the dining table, I had put a long red string reaching from one side of the wall to the other, and on this line, all my postcards were on display. There were Buddha statues from Thailand, the Golden Gate Bridge in San Francisco, the Colosseum in Rome, flowers from Holland, quotes from Germany, Russian churches and Japanese mountains. Some of the places we had visited, especially those in Europe because the flights were cheaper, but we wanted to see so many more places. It would all happen one day.

I still felt rough, but I wanted to hang out with Ajinder. If I went to her house, I would not have to cook. Bella could watch the Disney Channel, something I did not have at home. On the drive, we quickly stopped at the small supermarket to get some flowers for Ajinder.

FRIDAY, 6:30 PM

Ajinder's flat was in one of the modern housing estates. Each flat looked the same; everything was neat. Very little character. The places were purpose-built and reasonably priced. Ajinder's family had a downstairs flat with a small garden, which was amazing in the summer. I had spent many nights there with wine and great food as the kids played in the garden or watched TV inside. Bella ran towards the door and rang the bell; the buzzer went almost immediately. We walked along the yellow communal corridor towards Ajinder's flat. Number 4, here we were. The door was already open. I smelled Daal. Ajinder was a mind reader.

Her kids were in the living room, and as soon as Bella walked in, Ajinder's son Manpreet turned on the Disney Channel.

"Hey, Bella, do you want to watch TV with Avani?"

Avani jumped up and hugged Bella. She was two years older than Bella and had the brightest eyes. Ajinder and I walked towards the kitchen next to the living room.

"Thank god it's Friday."

Harkiran, Ajinder's husband, was still at work. He was a paramedic, worked shifts, and was not expected to be home until much later. Harkiran was a lovely guy. He and Ajinder matched very well. Their temperament was similar. Both loved eating, and it showed, but they were always bubbly and inviting. I loved coming over, whether Harkiran was in or not. Sometimes, when he was out, Ajinder would tell me about her first marriage and her family, with whom she had little contact since the divorce. It had taken Ajinder a few years to build herself a little community of colleagues and friends from university. At 39, she was in love and happy.

Tonight's main topic was the blow job incident from Tuesday morning. Apparently, Sunjit had been internally excluded for three days, so would be back in my lesson next Tuesday, hopefully, with a bit more restraint than this week. I had to share the newfound information about Gemma from finance and Mr Josiah. Neither of us was surprised. He was not called Casanova for nothing. It would all come out one day, and his mother-in-law would probably not want to see him again on her birthday or any other day. Then he could give Gemma from Finance more time, but it would probably become too dull, and he would move on to someone else. I wondered how Mr Josiah's watch reacted to his extracurricular engagements. At the moment, probably not much, considering it had been smashed in the morning, but on average, did his little affairs help his health? Who knew?

"Have a cup of tea and some biscuits whilst I cook," Ajinder demanded.

Manpreet joined us briefly before asking whether he could go to the cinema after dinner to meet his friends.

"Manpreet, my dear, as long as you are back before midnight, that's fine."

Ajinder made fresh chapatis whilst I prepared the salad. Half an hour later, the kids and I sat around the big dining table and enjoyed this delicious meal. Shortly after Avani and Bella indulged more in their TV show, Manpreet set off to the cinema. Ajinder and I continued gossiping and dreaming up plans to escape the factory, eating cake and having more tea. Ajinder was thinking about applying to private schools. Although she only worked three days, she felt she was forever working, even on her days off. Previously, Ajinder had been opposed to working in private schools, thinking she wanted to help the average kids. She had realised that even part-time teaching in state factories killed her, so she might as well try to work in private factories. At least the pay was a bit better, and the holidays were substantially longer.

"I can see myself and Bella living abroad."

"You are already abroad."

We both laughed.

"Another, new abroad."

"Where would you go?"

"The Middle East or Asia. Somewhere warm and sunny."

"Oh yes. That sounds like I want to join you. But you know what I find off-putting," Ajinder said, "the whole application process is too much work."

"Exactly. The factories keep serfs so busy that we have no time to apply elsewhere."

"There should be one format, like a pool where everyone can upload their CV and a supporting statement."

"Yes, every place has a different format, every factory wants your details in a different form. Why were CVs even invented?"

"Yes, for teaching jobs, a CV is utterly useless. And don't even get me started on the supporting statement."

"I will need a day off just to write that one."

We kept laughing, but it was not funny. Someone needed to be jobless to find a new job.

"Don't forget the action words, Eva. Action words are needed, nobody wants to look like a loser teacher. You must launch initiatives, lead a team, improve results, manage, etc."

"With data and evidence, proven track record."

"And before you apply, ask all the referees for a permission slip." Ajinder reminded us.

"Yes, that does not sit well with me. As soon as the overlords hear you are applying, you are an outcast in most factories."

"Tell me about it. You can only apply somewhere when you are ready to leave with or without a new job because the overlords will make your life hell."

"That makes it even harder. Who can just drop their job?"

"Rich people or those with rich partners or girls with sugar daddies."

"Well, that's us stuck in the factory forever."

"You know what I found exhausting, too?" Ajinder asked.

"Enlighten me. I find all of it exhausting."

"Interview day."

We slapped our legs simultaneously. Ajinder was right.

"Ah, don't get me started," I shook my head, "school tour, observation, panel interview, head interview, kids' interview, marking activity, data analysis activity."

"The kids' interview really is a joke, isn't it."

"You know James in Year 9, he told me a few months ago that he and some other kids selected the new science teacher."

"Yeah, right mate, that's what the overlords tell the kids." Ajinder laughed.

"It's all a show, student's voice and stuff, OFSTED tick box."

"I am always so tired when I come home from an interview. The observation is draining too because you don't know any of the kids," Ajinder complained, "and even if the factory gives you data, you don't know who is who."

I got up and went to check on the girls. They looked tired, and I thought it was best to leave before Bella fell asleep on the sofa. Ajinder put some leftovers in a container for us. On the way out, I reminded Ajinder that she had promised to pick up Bella on Monday, as she went to the same primary factory as Avani.

"No worries, we will take Bella with us on Monday after school, won't we, Avani?"

The girls were already excited to have another afternoon and evening together.

"Thank you so much for having us."

Bella joined in the hugging and goodbyes, and with that, they drove off into the night.

FRIDAY, 11:52 PM

We made it home before midnight. Bella had already fallen asleep in the car. I carried her inside, shut the door as quietly as possible and put her to bed. Then I sat down on the sofa, tired but happy. I sat there for 30 minutes staring at the ceiling before deciding it was time for a glass of Japanese whiskey. I often did that, just sat down and stared at the walls. The feeling of complete nothingness. And although I was tired, I was also wound up, unable to sleep yet. I turned on YouTube and started to watch a true crime documentary about some murder committed in America. For me, it had to be America, on a few occasions, I allowed myself to watch Australian crime, but only sometimes. I was a multi-tasker even when watching something. I never just sat and did one thing. I had to do something else, like write or read something online. For me, YouTube was almost like a podcast in the background.

I quickly looked at the teaching jobs online and thought there had to be another way to make money. Recently, on one of my Friday night internet sessions, I read about influencers being offered £10,000 to go on holiday with someone and possibly engage in extracurricular activities. That sounded more doable than applying for another teaching job. I did not understand why the influencers in question had declined such an offer. Why would they do that? £10,000 was what I called a decent proposal. Decline £10,000 for a holiday in the sun and some extracurricular activities? My suitcase would have been packed, and my newly acquired British passport would be in my hand faster than anyone could say *take off*.

When I had been on holiday with guys in another life, I had usually paid half of everything. I had been conned. No more of that! There were guys out there who paid women to come with them on holiday. Where were they, and how could I find one? To get paid to travel, relax and visit the genital theme park, what could be better? I was disappointed in myself, but I no longer would accept the below-standard holidaying. From now on I would go on holiday but I would charge. I wanted to be the beneficiary of this constructed fantasy. The only problem was finding someone to pay me. Actually, a second problem could have been the teacher standards. Was accepting payment for holidays fiddling at the margins of upholding the profession in the public eye? I was too tired to worry. Maybe the whiskey had gone to my head. Having watched or better listened to American true crime documentaries until nearly 2 am, I dismissed the idea of applying anywhere. I went to bed and fell asleep immediately.

SATURDAY, 8:15 AM

Listening to the silence, I sat down with my freshly made coffee. Looking down on myself. My T-shirt had a colossal lion with sunglasses on it. I was trying to remember how I got into this outfit. The sun shone on my face, and I decided today would be a good day. After gymnastics, Bella would go to her dad's. She had not seen him in seven weeks. Not because he was ill, working or in his home country, no, he just had not made time to see his daughter. There was no news there.

I started making pancakes, and shortly after, Bella looked around the corner, looking tired but smiling.

"I smell pancakes."

"Good morning, young lady, you are promoted to sniffer dog. Would you like a hot chocolate baby?"

"Yes, please, Mami. Today, Abbu will pick me up, Mami!"

"Have you packed your bag yet?"

"No, I will do it after breakfast. Do you think he

will be on time?"

"I am sure he will try. Sometimes, there is a lot of traffic."

I knew very well that he was never on time, and today would not be any different. We indulged in our pancakes with sugar and lemon. Then Bella quickly packed her bag, and we left the house for her gymnastics session. It was a nice little walk under the sun, or better for Bella, it was a skip. Like most Saturdays, she used her skipping rope to move. I followed, enjoying the warm air. Summer would soon be here. My favourite season. We walked past dog walkers in the park and spotted a few runners, some with Mr Josiah's gadget around their wrists.

When we arrived, Bella entered first. On two small benches in some sort of makeshift entrance area, where they were already, all the coupled-up parents. For some mums, those Saturday mornings were mini-dates. Some dads clearly did not want to be there. Watching the kids tumble and hop, what else could one do on a Saturday morning? While waiting for the first gymnastics session to finish, Elsa's mum overexcitedly greeted me.

"Good morning Eva, how are you? How is work? Soon, it's half-term and a few months later, a long summer break."

"I am alright. Busy with exam preparation and teaching."

I wanted to add a few more things but was not in the mood for *teachers to have a 12-week holiday* conversation with a housewife who had a rich husband and who had clearly fallen for the legend of the lazy teacher myth. I did not remember the name of this mum, but I remembered her ginger-haired daughter. The little girl was lovely and kind. Judging by her outfit, she clearly loved unicorns. Bella and Elsa started talking about some show from the Disney Channel, which I figured was great because it took the focus off me.

I did not like to entertain small talk. I thought of it as the biggest misapplication of language. Inauthentic chitter-chatter to fill the silence. I had zero tolerance for mind-numbing talk about the weather, kids' activities or food. Small talk scored equally as high as looking at someone's holiday photos. When the conversation was meaningful and about politics, human rights, sex, puppies or a revolution, I could be counted on. It was not that I lacked small talk skills. I simply hated it. My selfish gene did not care about someone's momentary thoughts.

I felt far more inclined to talk to people when I was younger. Back then, I was a people pleaser. These days, I was a calculating people pleaser when it meant keeping my job or getting something I wanted.

Finally, tiny Dorothy walked over in her red jogging trousers and pink t-shirt. She was the coach but gave the impression of a kind granny who would look after the kids for the morning. I did not know how long Dorothy had coached kids, but she and her husband Gary, who helped her run the club, seemed very established in the community. They also appeared to know everyone's business.

"Have a great time, Bella. I am off to the shopping centre," I said, "I will pick you up in an hour."

"OK, Mami, have fun."

I felt the stares of the super mums and Instagram couples as I walked out of the gym. I hardly ever stayed. I had been a gymnast in my younger years, and I could not remember any parent ever sitting there. Parents were at work or enjoyed their free time. On Saturdays, when Bella had gymnastics, I ran the errands I had no time for during my week, unlike Elsa's mum.

Rumi had told me about Postcrossing a year or so ago. It seemed a great way of seeing the world without travelling, which would be pretty pricey. With Postcrossing, I got postcards from strangers from around the world, and I sent strangers postcards, too. That is why the visit to the post office was crucial. I wanted to spend the time Bella went to her dad's to write some postcards. As I waited in line, I noticed a lot of noise from one of the counters. Everyone started to look over and tried to listen in to what the scene was about. It was impossible not to pay attention because the old man in the wheelchair kept kicking a lady and waving a walking stick around. I thought it was probably just a frustrated pensioner. Suddenly, there was a loud crash from the entrance area. The door to the post office had been broken. Glass shattered everywhere, including on the old man in the wheelchair and the lady with him. I left the queue to see if they were alright. Two other customers followed me, as did a lady who worked there.

"Are you alright? Are you hurt?" The post office lady asked.

I was shocked, not by the strength of the old man in the wheelchair who must have smashed the door with his waving walking stick, but by his companion. The lady who had pushed the wheelchair and asked the old man to be quiet just minutes ago was Mrs Viper, the CEO of my factory. She looked ashamed and embarrassed, with tears in her eyes.

"I am so sorry, my father has Alzheimer's. Today is not a good day," she whispered to the post office lady, "what can I do to clear this up and pay for it?"

Her father now looked very much like a different person. Within seconds, his demeanour had changed, and he looked like an innocent old little man.

"Are you sad?" He asked his daughter.

"Don't worry, we will take care of it."

"Thank you. Let me leave my phone number just in case."

Mrs Viper scribbled her number on a piece of paper. She handed it to the lady from the post office. Only then did she notice me and nod in acknowledgement. I nodded back, hoping my mouth was no longer open. Mrs Viper turned around and held onto the wheelchair.

"Let's go, dad. Please give me your walking stick. I will carry it."

I felt downcast. This was a sad incident to have witnessed. It was even sadder because I had never thought of Mrs Viper as a person outside the factory, someone with problems at home. Someone with a real life. I returned to the queue. As people had now left, I did not have to wait long.

I left the post office and returned to the gym with my ten international stamps. I saw Mrs Viper and her dad near the car park on my way. She looked like a different person. There was no confidence in this woman. Her shoulders hung. She looked exhausted, even from this far away.

This was not the boss lady I knew.

Bella's session had just come to an end.

"Mami, Mami, come on, let's go home. Abbu is coming soon."

She could not contain her excitement.

"How was gymnastics baby Bella? What new moves did you learn?"

"Nothing new, Mami. I was just practising my floor routine. Dorothy said that we have a competition next month."

"Wow, that sounds exciting. Let's ask Abbu to come along, what do you think?"

"Yeah, we will ask him."

Bella skipped ahead of me excitedly. I could not get the post office incident out of my head. At home, we had some leftover food Ajinder had given us last night. Bella sat by the front window, waiting for her dad to arrive, like a puppy waiting for its owner. I sat with her for a short while, looking out the window. Opposite, the husband from *hubby jobs*' house cleaned his car. I thought that this was a typical sunshine activity. Cleaning the car on a Saturday. For some men, it was almost like making love. Great care ensured every centimetre of the car's surface was caressed like a beautiful woman. Adult film directors could use this as a professional development study. There was a lot to learn here. Most men used a variety of products which could rival a teenage girl's beauty product collection. Bottles of green and pink magic potions were applied. The vehicle's skin was lavishly shampooed, conditioned and rigorously polished. Like a curvy bum, the bonnet was eyed up from different angles and polished more for good measure. It was an incredible display of affection, attention and love. Sadly, it was directed at a thing.

Lay people like me felt the rain would do the job of car washing. I thought that washing a car was like cleaning shoes. Pointless. It was a waste of energy. A six-monthly look around the interior and a nice air freshener on the rearview mirror would suffice. No need for a 45-minute love-making session. But for the hardcore car wash guys, washing a car became a concerted event. A car had to be freed from the dust of the filthy town. It needed to shine in sterile splendour, like a virgin car from the showroom. The more expensive the car, the more endurance the owner showed in cleaning it. I wanted to know whether the same scrutiny was given to cleaning the toilet or oven.

When I was little, kids used to clean cars. Sometimes, dads and kids would do the cleaning together. That was now a no-no. It had become an exclusively male activity. For some guys, it was probably an excuse not to spend time with their family and opt out of carrying any mental load that came with having kids and running a household.

SATURDAY, 2 PM

There was still no sign of Bella's dad, no message. This was nothing new. He was never on time, blaming traffic or forgetting that he had promised to pick up Bella. I found it odd that there was never any traffic when I took Bella to her dad. The traffic must only have been in one direction.

"Do you think Abbu is stuck in traffic, Mami?"

"I think so."

I decided to call him. I went to the kitchen, where my phone was charging on the table. No answer. The phone seemed to be switched off. He was meant to be here over an hour ago, but knowing him, he was probably still on his snore shelf.

"Hey, Baby Bella, how about we go to Camden Market? If we leave now, we can be there by around 3.30," I suggested," I can tell Abbu that we are coming to London, and he can pick you up from there, what do you think?"

"Camden Market, where the people in crazy clothes walk around?" Bella asked excitedly, remembering the woman dressed like a fairy and when this old man walked around in Victorian clothing.

"Yes, that place. Abbu can meet us there. At least we can still have fun."

"Yes, Mami, let me get my bag."

We went to London often because it was only 40 minutes on the train, and Bella's dad lived there. She had been born in West London, and I had lived there a few years before Bella arrived. We both loved Camden. Bella liked looking at the jewellery, art and fashion, and I just came for the atmosphere and because it reminded me of when I first came to live in London many years ago when I worked as an Au Pair in North London and spent most of my weekends in Camden. The unusual shops, unconventional people, the dress sense, and the food were all exciting.

The weather was glorious, and rather than jumping on the Northern Line, we decided to walk from King's Cross Station all the way to Camden, but only after buying a cupcake. It had to be the blueberry vanilla one and a coffee for me. With our rations in hand, we set off. We passed the British Library, turned right by Euston Station, and went straight along the housing estate and Mornington Crescent Station.

As always, it was buzzing. There was Spanish

and German chatter from school groups all around us. Although busy, I did not care because people just minded their business. Nobody tried to make unnecessary conversation with anyone. Our first stop was the food market around the Amy Winehouse statue. We found a little corner of a bench, and Bella sat on my lap, surrounded by food smells and tourists from around the globe. My phone rang, and I handed my food box to Bella, whispered, "Abbu," and picked up the phone.

"Ami, how are you? Where are you? Sorry, but I had to work late and overslept. I only just woke up. Where should I meet you?"

Bella's dad spoke as if nothing had happened.

"We are in Camden. How about you meet us here in an hour?"

"Ah, Camden, that will take ages to get to now. Why don't you drop Bella off at mine?"

"No, I need to go back home. How about you meet us at King's Cross Station in two hours?"

"Well, that would work. See you. Give Bella a kiss from me."

He put the phone down. I smiled at Bella.

"Abbu will come to King's Cross Station and pick you up later. How cool is that?"

Bella beamed.

"Very cool."

SATURDAY, 5:30 PM

I was disappointed in this baby daddy. He was meant to be at our house at lunchtime. He had only just woken up. Sometimes, I wondered what would happen if I died and Bella had to live with her dad. Would he get her to school, help her with homework, take her to gymnastics, organise dentist appointments and attend parents' evenings? He had never done any of those things because he had a degree in excuses. I could under no circumstances die before Bella was 18, maybe 16, that could work. Those thoughts depressed me.

"Bella, tell me what we are looking at next?"

She pointed to the little little shop by the corner.

"Mami, please, can you get me some juggling balls? And can you teach me also?"

"I think that's possible. Maybe you can learn some tricks and work at the circus."

"You could work at the circus, too."

I wanted to say that I was working at the circus already.

"Which job would I do at the circus?"

"You could balance on a tightrope."

"Yes, but only if it was less than two feet above the ground. You know that I don't like heights."

There were three balls in a small colourful box. Bella did not want a bag because she wanted to squish the new balls on her way to King's Cross. I paid by card, thinking cash would soon disappear.

"Can I have your email address, please?"

"My email? Why?"

"For the receipt."

"No."

I felt slightly sorry for the guy who had to ask for my email. He had a pen-pusher boss and was probably on a zero-hour contract, and maybe he even had some stupid target and got shamed in a WhatsApp staff group for not getting enough email addresses.

Bella took her juggling balls.

"Mami, why did the man ask for your email address?"

"So that his boss has it, and then the company will keep sending me emails."

"But isn't it nice to get emails," Bella wanted to know, "like getting postcards?"

"It is lovely to get postcards and letters from friends and family, but emails from companies are very boring," I explained, "they just want you to buy new things."

I did not like email receipts, but paper receipts had equally become a nuisance. Email receipts were being sold as environmentally friendly, and I got that. But I also thought the environment was of little concern to many CEOs. They were not defenders of the environment but commercial stalkers.

Back to King's Cross Station, it was less busy than on our way to Camden. There was no sign of Bella's dad. So, we sat in the square, and I showed Bella how to juggle. 20 minutes later, Bella spotted her dad walking towards us, dropped her juggling balls and ran right into his arms. She was overjoyed. I got up, too and collected all of Bella's belongings together.

"Hi, how are you?"

"Great, how about you?"

Turning to Bella, he said, "Did you have a great time in Camden?"

"Yes, Abbu, I got new juggling balls."

"Why don't you show me later how well you can juggle already?"

"Bella, I have to catch the train now. I will see you tomorrow evening," I hugged her. "Have a great time with Abbu. Give me a big hug and kiss, please."

"I will drop Bella tomorrow evening. Ammi, have a nice evening. You can party tonight."

He smiled a stupid smile.

I walked towards the station entrance, ready to smack someone. Party? Yes, party for one with takeaway and an early night. These comments were part of his repertoire. He repeated them every time, along with saying I did not need child support because I earned good money. I took all this crappy talk and did not comment because I knew it was pointless. It would not stop, and I was here for Bella and not myself. One day, when Bella was older, I would be free from this nonsense. Bella loved her dad. She was too young to understand that her dad did not live up to expectations financially or emotionally. I was tired of having to call him every month for £100 or £150. When he was utterly useless, I had to be nice to him, but I was too tired to take this money business to court. It would probably cost me more than I would gain.

In the station, the regular Londoners were, as usual, rushing rather than walking. This is how I could spot the tourists, not by their maps or cameras, both of which formed part of anyone's phone these days, but by them stopping suddenly, looking and commenting at something, and being extra slow.

SATURDAY, 8 PM

I was back home with a Matar Paneer and Chicken Biryani from my local Indian restaurant, trying to find something interesting to watch on TV. But there was nothing. Why did I pay for this TV licence? The authorities certainly thought it was necessary. I wished upskirting, assault or not paying child support were taken as seriously as not paying this silly TV licence fee. A few years ago, I was harassed by the TV licence police. They repeatedly sent me letters, and I kept letting them know that I neither watched TV nor did I own a TV. In an Orwellian moment, the TV licence police ended up at my door one evening. I was too happy to show them my little flat had no TV equipment. I was doing my teacher's training. There was no time for TV, radio, fun or entertainment. Adding a five-year-old into the mix, there was no time for anything. They finally accepted that I was a weirdo who did not indulge in soaps and sports and left me alone.

I really did not see the value of it. £157.50 for what? I used online streaming services, which I had already paid for. The news coverage was not worth much compared to other international stations. At least they should have used my fee to invest in a training session on questioning for journalists. I could have run this session as I did so on Tuesday in the factory anyway. Some of their journalists really let themselves down because their questioning was poor. If serfs questioned students and how those journalists questioned politicians, the inspectors and overlords would have a field day and wipe the floor with us. But they did that anyway. My family abroad watched more BBC World Service than I watched BBC. I was financing their TV! Another thing that wound me up was the money paid to some of their *top people.* I did not think those sums were justified. This was entertainment, not brain surgery. Where were the serial killers, human rights documentaries, authentic sex scenes including period sex and programmes about sharks? That was what I happily would have paid for.

In the end, as on most nights, I found some true crime documentaries on Netflix, and the description of a savage killing ate my dinner while trying to stay awake. My phone kept buzzing. Rumi was on a roll sending videos all evening. When I was about to go to bed, she wanted to know if I wanted to meet her in town for some shisha. I lied, stating I was already in bed, and Rumi accepted but reminded me that we had booked the Moonlight restaurant in North London in two weeks. I sent a thumbs up and hoped Rumi would forget.

Although I liked this place, it took a lot of work to get to. I could not be bothered by the fake queues outside those restaurants either. Those places did not let anyone book a table. This would have been too easy, too common sense. They loved queues outside so that they could pretend everyone fancied their food. Usually, a 20-something underpaid art student with green hair would jump at us with an iPad and excitedly ask how they could help. With a huge and insincere grin, they would then announce a 50-minute wait. Add another 30 before we could start eating. It was all a show, almost like a script that call centre staff follow. It was always 50 minutes, never 35 or 1 hour, no 50 minutes. What a terrible waste of people's time. After another hour of crime, I ensured the windows and doors were locked and went off to bed, falling asleep quickly.

SUNDAY, 10 AM

Beep. Beep. Beep.
Beep. Beep. Beep.

Panic set in. Half asleep, I made it to the door in my dressing gown, unable to open my eyes properly. I had not ordered anything on Amazon. Who could be here in the early hours of Sunday? I opened the door.

"Good morning, Mami."

I froze. Did I sleep all day? Was it already the evening? I could not even speak yet.

"Mama, I brought you some paratha for breakfast."

"Ammi, how was the party? Must have been a long party if you are still not up."

I detected another stupid grin on his face.

"Bye, bye my beautiful beti, see you soon. Love you."

"Bye, Abbu, I love you too."

Bella waved. She ran to the window, waving a bit more before her dad drove off. That was it. My little break was over before it had even begun. It had just turned 10 am. The dad had looked after Bella for around 13 hours in the last seven weeks. Superdad, we should get him a medal. I tried to find my bearings. Before I could shut the door, overweight James, who lived next to Elizabeth, also had to get on my nerves.

"Good morning Eva, are you ready for the half-term? Must be nice to be a teacher."

He went to his car, giggling. I was still unresponsive, which was good because otherwise, I would have called him an idiot. For him facts were optional. I was not awake enough to hand out a verbal slap to Bella's father and his stupid party enquiry. Neither was I quick enough to respond to James, who drank too much, especially when his football team played. Those who thought teaching was a walk in the park should give up their jobs and try it for a week. I had known people who went back to corporate jobs after short stunts in teaching because it was too stressful to be a serf.

"So, Baby Bella, how are you on this glorious morning? Thank you for the paratha and for bringing more sunshine."

I had to be a parent now. This self-indulgence had to stop immediately.

"Mami, it was so much fun at Abbu's house. We ordered pizza, had lots of Fanta, and went out at 11 o'clock, Mami, 11 at night to buy ice cream."

"Wow, this sounds amazing."

"I will make us some fried eggs with this paratha," I said, "but first, I will just jump in the shower quickly, ok?"

Bella was practising with her juggling balls again. How was the night over so quickly? Where had it gone? I stood under the shower, shampooing my hair. The hot water was running down my back and legs. My showers were always too hot, nearly causing burns, but that was fine. This was how I liked it: hot, just like my summers, just like I liked my bacon carbonated and steak well done. I liked most things hot and burnt.

I was back, feeling refreshed and clean, ready to start this day. I warmed up the paratha, made some eggs, and made a giant cup of coffee and hot chocolate for Bella.

"Are you excited that your grandpa is coming soon to take you on holiday with grandma?".

"Yippie, Mami, what is the best food in Austria?"

I thought, that's my girl, that's how I knew Bella was my baby. This was the piece of evidence that was not needed. We both loved our food.

"Kaiserschmarrn and Apfelstrudel," I said, "do you want to invite someone for a sleep-over when you return from Austria because it will be half-term?"

Having a spare kid friend over meant more

free time for me because the two kids would be busy with each other.

"Yes, Mami, I want to ask if Angel can come over."

"Awesome, you ask Angel, and if she wants to come, I will call her mum, and we will sort it all out."

The telly was turned on, and Bella lazed on the sofa, occasionally getting up to get a bounty bar or crisps. I sat down with my postcards. The first card I had to send was to Ivan in Belarus. He sounded interesting, a university student who liked to play the guitar and walk his two dogs. I wrote part of the card in Russian, which I still remember from my school days when I had to learn it as a foreign language. The other postcards were for people in China, Germany and the Netherlands. I also had to start climbing Mount Everest of marking. Green words had to go into the two piles of books I had carried home on Friday evening and ignored until now. I needed a lot more coffee to get through this before dinner.

SUNDAY, 2:15 PM

In Bella's school bag, I found a tennis-sized ball of paper. She had the habit of folding paper into the most miniature shapes. I started to worry whether this was some psychological problem. Being surrounded by psychological reports and training sessions on special educational needs, anxiety and depression, I could easily see a problem in any behaviour. Having unfolded this paper and removed the creases with my flat hand several times, I realised it was a letter from the school. Bella's blouse did not adhere to the school uniform standards; please ensure her uniform followed the school's uniform rules, it said. That was odd. It was the middle of May. Bella wore the same blouses from the same company all year round. I was sure it was the school uniform shop I got them from. I opened Bella's little wardrobe and took out one of the green hangers with a school blouse on it. The label clearly stated *school uniform shop*. A triumph for me.

I opened my laptop and compiled a nice little email to Bella's factory to be sent to whoever may be in charge of school uniform issues. I explained that this was the same blouse Bella had worn all year, it was clearly labelled *uniform* and that I would not buy a new blouse for the last eight weeks of term. I refused to buy a new uniform because Bella would grow over the summer. And to top it all off, I took a picture of the *uniform shop* label and attached it. Bella's factory should leave me alone. Her attendance was fine, her behaviour was no problem, and she made good progress. This would have to do. The factory should try to find a real problem.

I returned to Bella's bag and found another second paper ball. This one was slightly bigger. A birthday invitation. It was for a week from a boy called Jordan. I did not remember having heard this name before. If people did not know a child's name, that child was an average child who let people get on with their lives. The average was a great place to be. Bella would already be in Austria, so I would not get to know this mysterious Jordan. It did not matter. There would be enough other kids as the whole group had most likely been invited, as was standard procedure for kids' parties. All the kids had to be friends, like each other, and invite each other to parties. Nobody was left behind. The kids were all soldiers. They would carry their upset peers over their shoulders like war veterans carried their injured peers away from the battlefield, only the kids' battlefield was the playground.

Having kids these days meant either being broke or insane or likely both. The inconvenient fact was there would be 30 parties per year. 30 Saturdays straight in the bin. Not only did the parent have to ferry the kid to the party, but in most places, the parent was expected to stay to show face and smile along this charade. An epicentre for suicidal thoughts. What was even worse was there was no alcohol at those parties. How was anyone meant to survive this? Some people on Fantasy Island were convinced that drinking in front of small people would turn the cutie pies into deviant alcoholics. This reminded me of the holiday in Malaga, where the playground had a bar for the parents. Thank you, Spain. I was delighted at the time. Bella climbed the climbing frames, picking up kiddie Spanish, and I sat by the side, having a glass of wine. Similar arrangements existed in many European towns. That was what I called family-friendly. Gone were the days of subcontracted weekend childcare, when one would drop their small person at a party, zoom home for uninterrupted extra-curricular activities, and zoom back just in time for the party parents to not call social services for forgetting to pick up a child. It was probably even worse for people with two or more kids. Game over. These parents were kids' party captives. For them, the asylum was calling.

"Bella, let's put the postcards on the line," I said towards the sofa where Bella was still relaxing and watching TV. Bella went straight for the tiny pink pegs, which I kept in a jar on the fridge. I had to help her because she could not reach the top of the fridge even by standing on her toes.

"Here you go."

One after the other, Bella hung up the postcards we had received on Friday.

"Do you like it?"

"No, I love it, just like you."

SUNDAY, 8 PM

I handed Bella the plates so she could set the table. Someone knocked at the door as we sat down to eat our dinner.

"Eva, here are the keys."

“When will you be back?"

"Next Saturday," Elizabeth replied, "Thank you for watering the plants."

"No problem. Do you want to have dinner with us? We have sausages, mash and Sauerkraut."

"Thank you for the offer, but I'm meeting a friend for dinner."

"Have a wonderful time, Elizabeth."

We enjoyed dinner and dessert: rice pudding with lots of sugar, cinnamon, and apple puree. After dinner, Bella wanted to write a story but did not know how to start.

"Which story don't you like, Bella?"

"The frog prince," Bella said without hesitation, "I would never want to kiss a frog."

"Me neither."

"It's disgusting."

"So why don't you change the story around, how would the Frog Prince be a better story?"

"If the frog was a puppy. That would be cute."

"I agree. A puppy is much cuter than a frog," I said, "why don't you write your story whilst I do the dishes?"

I went to the kitchen to tidy up.

"Bella, how is the story going?"

"I am done, Mami, can I read it to you?

"How about that? You get ready for bed, and then you read me your story as a good night story?"

Thirty minutes later, Bella climbed onto her bed, and rather than lying down, she stood on it and started to read her little story.

"Once upon a time, there was a clever girl. Her name was Isabel. She had a little puppy called Kitty. Kitty was cute and fluffy. Every day when Isabel came home from school, she would kiss Kitty on the nose, and then Kitty turned into a little girl who would play with Isabel in her room. Whenever Isabel heard her mum or dad walk up the stairs, she quickly kissed Kitty on the nose, and then Kitty turned back into a puppy."

I clapped, "Wow, Bella, what a fabulous story. Wouldn't it be great if it were to be true?"

"Yes, that would be amazing. I would never go to school but play with Kitty all day."

With Bella in bed, all books marked, I turned on the TV to check the news, but I went straight for a TV channel based in Qatar. Here, real news was delivered. By journalists who asked difficult questions. No celebrity gossip, no mid-level politician rambling their way through a scripted interview, no-nonsense. Here was a mixing desk of information. I learnt about someone being put on trial for human rights violations. There was talk about the military presence of several countries in the South China Sea. I was educated about the conflict over oil in Libya. I witnessed actual interviews with scary questions without this contaminated unicorn fluff, which was applied to appease people. Guests had a meaningful debate, like mature grown-ups. They showed respect for other people's ideas. Those guys were not tone-deaf. It was fascinating and refreshing. I watched it for half an hour with my mouth wide open and wondered why those programmes were never shown here. Indeed, this type of programme existed years ago but was somehow banished. But this was enough news now; I had to use my time wisely. I could manage at least two episodes of Criminal Minds and further develop my forensic analysis skills, although I already considered myself an honorary team member.

MONDAY, 6:05 AM

Bella's right foot rested on my belly. She must have snuck into the bedroom during the night. I had not noticed it. She did this when monsters hid behind her curtains. There was no need to wake her just yet. I carefully moved her foot and crawled out of bed. On my way to the bathroom, I turned on the kettle. Through the bathroom window, I noticed the blue sky. The weather looked lovely, but who knew what it would be like near Dudley? Once I sat down with my freshly made coffee, I checked my phone for any overnight catastrophes, but apart from a few cute, funny videos and some feminist memes sent by Rumi, nothing had happened.

"Good morning, Mami," a sleepy voice declared from around the corner.

Tired, Bella crawled straight onto my lap, putting her head on my left shoulder. She tried to continue to sleep.

"Baby Bella, tell me how you ended up in my bed last night."

"Mami, I think there was a unicorn that

kidnapped me." Bella giggled.

For a few minutes, we sat there doing nothing.

Like a penguin, Bella wobbled into the bathroom. I finished my coffee, toasted some bread and warmed up the beans. I got my grey backpack, the one that had been to most European cities and always went on school trips, and filled it with sandwiches, some cake, a few apples, water and lots of sweets and biscuits. When I went on school trips, my bag weighed equal my weekly shop. There was always the danger of getting stuck in traffic in the middle of nowhere. Although we were meant to be back by 6 pm, there was no guarantee. Bella walked in, looking shocked.

"Mami, why are you taking all this food with you?"

"Baby, you know Mami is a food monster. And also, I am going to Dudley, to a museum with lots of kids. Remember, I told you last week," I said, "that's why you are going home with Ajinder. I will pick you up from her house."

"This is the food monster house."

We set off earlier than usual because I had to see a few people before getting on the coach. I went through a list in my head, thinking about what else I had to do or might need to remember. These trips were in no way relaxing. They generated a tremendous amount of work before they had even taken off, often longer than the official work day and usually had some measure of drama nobody wanted. I held Bella's hand, and we walked into the breakfast club together. Bella was still yawning.

"Good morning, Mrs Shah, how was your weekend?"

I hoped there would be a short answer. I had no time for chit-chat.

"Yes, it was lovely. Good morning, Bella, how are you?"

"I am tired. I wish we could have another Sunday."

Mrs Shah and I nodded and smiled at each other. There was nobody to disagree with that.

"Mrs Shah, I am going on a school trip, and my friend and colleague will pick up Bella. Here are her details."

I gave her a form, which I had already completed at home. The after-school club would not just hand over a child to anyone who asked for one.

"Ah, I remember your friend Ajinder. Thank you for filling in the form already. Have a great trip. You will need another weekend after today."

I rolled my eyes in agreement. Bella's kisses started flying until we could not see each other anymore.

MONDAY, 8:05 AM

One thing I loved about trips was civilian clothing. I could just rock up in jeans, a T-shirt and a hoodie. Serfs and overlords still had to bring our high-vis, but I might conveniently leave it on the coach. The kids had another idea about trip attire. Any time they were allowed civilian clothing, a fashion show followed as sunshine followed the rain.

It was challenging to navigate into the car park. There were already six coaches parked outside and plenty of kids looking as if they were attending a wedding. This was precisely what I had expected. Some girls had arrived in the most glamorous but inappropriate outfits because non-uniform trips meant time to show off. This morning was no different. Some kids were ready for Milan but not the mines.

Mike was by the gate. He tried to disperse the crowd of kids gathering. I wriggled my Corsa through and stopped next to some fancy convertible car. It was Mr Cunningham's car, the overlord in charge of data or, officially known, Assistant Headteacher for Curriculum and Assessment. I liked this overlord the least, but not so much because he was evil. He probably was not, but everything about him irritated me, starting from his banker suits over this stupid car, how he carried himself, and how he took his job far too seriously. He did not need a car because he lived in the factory. He hardly left the place. No wonder he had to find a relationship within the factory. Monica was an early career mathematics teacher who had just started in September. They had become an item pretty quickly. Although both kept denying it, it was blatantly apparent as they could always be seen together in the factory, and if he finally chose to leave, she was often with him. I did not understand how someone in their early 30s could be so old in the head. I felt like scratching this dumb car with my key.

The reception area was busy with people. It was the norm on trip days. I had to push past several people who were not involved in the trip but had to take up space in the entrance area pretending to have something to contribute. Because trips also meant half-digested food on seats which no coach driver, teacher or anyone else on the coach enjoyed, I wanted to organise some bin liners. I walked along the corridor over to Carlos's storeroom. A collection of cleaning equipment, brooms, buckets and the bin liners I was after were neatly stocked in there.

"Carlos, how was your weekend?"

"Ah, Eva, it's a trip day. The weekend was wonderful. We booked our flights to Brazil."

Carlos pulled me closer towards him. He whispered, "We have decided to sell the house and move to Brazil. I am so happy."

With his left index finger, he covered his mouth. My eyes nearly popped out. I smiled and sealed my lips with an invisible key, which I threw into the air.

"What wonderful news. I will miss you, as I am sure many others here will, too."

I felt a mixture of happiness and sadness.

"Carlos, I need some bin liners. You know these kids eat everything, but their body cannot cope with being on a coach."

"I know what you mean," Carlos replied, on his toes stretching to reach the high shelves with the bin liners chuckling.

"The amount of junk food I have seen outside, I think we need to stock up on those bin liners."

I replied, wondering whether I had packed the Vicks tub in my bag. A hack I had learnt from Cara. It was the anti-gag reflex remedy when cleaning up kids' vomit. This was not what I had signed up for, but those kids needed to get out of their area. Seeing places farther away than two miles was necessary in an area where parents needed more cash.

Carlos turned around.

"Look, Eva, Louise made this for you. You can take it on the trip, but keep the kids from having it. We don't want it to end up in the bin liner."

We both laughed out loud. Carlos handed me a box.

"These coxinhas are shaped to resemble a drumstick or a little teardrop and are made from chicken stock, potatoes, shredded chicken and a soft cheese called requeijão and deep-fried."

"They look delicious and will keep me going. Thank you so much."

I left Carlos's store room and followed skinny Mr Cunningham. He was in civilian clothing and wore his high-vis jacket. This was not good news. He was probably going on our trip, too. This trip needed many supervisors. As the overlords did not teach much, they were sent on trips more than regular serfs. Fewer supply teachers needed to be booked, saving the school a lot of money. With everything being outsourced in a capitalist fashion, supply agencies made a killing by charging factories extortionate fees of which the supply serf would see a tiny fraction. If one of the supply teachers later managed to get a permanent job at a factory, the agency would charge the factory up to 14% of the annual salary in something they called a finder's fee. This was where taxes left hard-working people and moved into the pockets of pen pushers. Most kids would not do work unless their regular serfs were around; thus, this was an expensive babysitting service. But, of course, these agencies were praised for their entrepreneurial spirit by the people in power.

I was not looking forward to Cunnigham joining us as I suspected he would turn this whole trip into a military mission. I kept following him, and my heart sank. He did go outside straight to Mr Josiah, who was in charge of the trip, but would probably say nothing if Cunningham took over. By the gate, I spotted Ajinder, who had to park her car off the factory grounds. By now, so many kids were blocking the entrance that Mike could not move them along. Apart from Cunningham, there was no overlord out here to manage this overcrowded situation somehow. They were too busy chatting in the entrance area around reception.

"Look who is coming on the trip?" I indicated to Cunningham with my eyes.

Ajinder smiled.

"My condolences, Eva. With that fun machine on board, you will solve equations the whole journey."

"Thank you so much for looking after Bella this evening. I have let Mrs Shah know that you are coming. She remembered you."

"Try and have a nice day, and I'll see you tonight. I will have food ready for you."

I walked over to Cara, who was in the middle of giving some of the girls a telling-off.

"Where did you think you were going? To a wedding?"

The fashionistas remained silent.

"Ladies, we are going to the Black Country Museum. We will spend time in a mine. The rest of the time, we will walk around outside. Do you at least have a jacket?"

"No, Miss." One of the three wedding guests replied whilst the others shook their heads.

"OK, go to the lost property room and get yourself a jacket for the day." Cara looked at the girls sceptically. They moved away like puppies with their tails between their legs.

"Where are the parents? Don't they read the letters we send them? I am losing the will to live, and we have not even left the car park yet."

"It's the same every time. At least I have bin liners for any puke attacks later."

"Don't remind me of what is to come. I may not step on the coach."

Walking towards us was Louise, from the canteen. She and two other dinner ladies held huge crates carrying lunches for kids who typically had free school meals. The number of lunches made the deprivation of the catchment area visible. Half the kids on the roll were free school meal kids. Yet, by the end of the day, most of those lunches would go in the bin as kids refused to take them. A better way had to be found to distribute these meals on trip days. No kid wanted to be seen taking one.

The entire year 8 group, apart from a few kids with top-level behaviour issues, were going on this trip. This meant around 200 kids. They loved trips, and this one was extra special because it would last all day. Better still, it was a non-uniform trip. This was a long-haul, jet-lag-inducing adventure. For some kids, it would be their first time leaving their neighbourhoods. The boarding process was different from a RyanAir flight. Getting all the explorers in the correct groups onto the correct coaches took ages. The drivers were ever so patient. The first tears started rolling because a best friend suddenly decided to sit next to someone else. Nobody wanted to be close to a serf. Everyone forgot how to speak at an acceptable volume, shouting and screeching instead.

Sometimes, those trips with kids were hilarious, like when one kid on a day trip to France asked whether they had entered France after crossing over the Thames. It was apparent that trips were needed to widen horizons. Sadly, Cunnigham had been put on my coach, and as soon as he stepped on, the relaxed holiday atmosphere changed. The kids looked at each other, pulling faces reflecting what the serfs on board thought. They were stuck with this hedge fund manager overlord. He would probably give them tasks instead of leaving everyone to get on with their own business. Having completed the headcount three times, to assure myself and because the girls in the back kept screaming, I was satisfied that all the kids and staff meant to be on our coach were here. I ticked the register, got off the coach and walked back to reception to hand over the register to Flora.

Mr Josiah got off his coach, his green shake in one hand and the register in the other.

"Miss, aren't you excited? The Black Country Museum trip is one of my favourites. The kids will get so much out of it."

"Yes, it will be amazing." I lied.

At least I did not have to teach today. Instead, I had to make sure nobody got injured or lost. Reception Flora already had several other registers in her hand.

"Guys, you are the last two groups. Have a great day, and leave some of the kids there." She said sarcastically.

"Not on this trip, Flora, but when we go to the Tower of London, we will try," I replied.

Mr Josiah, walking down the steps, shook his head, "Ladies, stay professional, please."

Flora and I looked sceptical.

"Will you be counting steps, Sir?"

"Miss, you cannot believe what happened. My watch is the new watch I showed you on Friday.

It must have somehow come off. One of the girls found it, and it was completely trashed. I have not been able to track my steps, calories or sleep," his voice sounded worried, "I have no idea what my body is up to."

"Oh dear, well, I hope you can get it fixed," I said, turning towards my open coach door.

MONDAY, 9:20 AM

I counted three steps onto the coach. Interestingly, now that his gadget was broken, he looked more stressed than when constantly monitored. What a crazy world! I sat beside family man Frank, the factory's designated first aider and a maths teacher.

"Susanna is doing her GCSEs this year. She can sit them at our factory."

"Do you have to pay for her to sit as an external candidate? And which other subjects will she do?"

I was fascinated by the idea of homeschooling. Frank's three kids had all been through it. One was already at university. I never knew that homeschooling was an option on this island. Had I known it earlier, I might have considered it an option for Bella, but I would have had to find some cash or win the lottery. The occasional £150 per month donation from Bella's father would not have cut it. Several years in the factory and conversations with Frank completely changed my mind about homeschooling.

"Martha, my wife is a writer, she does English and Geography with the kids. For Spanish, we work with another family and hire a tutor. The kids do maths and science with me. I work four days per week, so it all works out for us as a family."

This sounded idyllic. There was another way for kids to be educated without the hidden agenda. Schooling in a relaxed environment without constant testing. Those parents were amazing, taking on all this responsibility for educating the kids and standing up against society's judgement. I had to admit that I used to be judgy, too. But by now, I was already nervous about Bella's secondary school. I saw the point. Being a serf in a factory did not help either. I knew what went on on the shop floor.

This whole factory choice issue was what I called an illusion, in fact, it was a lie. When the government and inspectors advocate factory inspections with ratings at the end of two days, they try to spin it in such a way as if the parents needed it. Without the inspection, there would be no way for parents to know how good or bad a factory was. It was necessary for making informed choices, they would say, completely ignoring that many parents out there did not get their first choice factory or even their second or third. It would be even more challenging if no older siblings were at the school. This whole rating and choice system needed to be revised. It did not work. And what about the kids that ended up in factories with a poor rating, they surely must have felt like they ended up in the bin. For some, there would be a self-fulfilling prophecy; having been sent to a poor school, some would become this label. Reaching the gold standard of *outstanding* came at a heavy human cost. The elite members' club in power, who had masterminded this scheme, shrugged at the collateral damage with courteous disinterest. The exhaustion caused by the search for perfection and ever-better exam results was accepted, tolerated and even expected. After all, serfs and kids had all the holidays to recover.

Behind us, the TikTok videos were blaring from each corner. Snapchat photos were taken. Selfies went through filters and editing processes that would make Hollywood jealous. Next to Emma, noisy Melanie had become quiet. Maybe because her ex-boyfriend Bradley sat with Aisha, or she would be the first to throw up. And just as I had completed this thought, Emma was waving.

"Miss, Miss, a bin liner, please."

The coach smell was replaced by the smell of undigested skittles and chocolate biscuits for the rest of the journey. My little blue tub of Vicks came in handy now.

MONDAY, 11:45 AM

It took around two hours to get to the museum. Cunningham took charge, as expected. He got all the kids and serfs to line up next to the coach and completed the head count. Then he started his little overlord trip speech.

"Students, please pay attention to what I am about to say. You are here as representatives of your school community. At all times, we expect you to follow our instructions and the staff's instructions on-site. This is a wonderful learning opportunity for you," he waved a pile of worksheets in his hand, "I have taken the liberty to create this worksheet for you. I expect all of you to complete this whilst in the museum."

He signalled to Cara and myself to come and hand them out. I glanced over the worksheet. Nearly 30 questions or tasks needed to be completed, and an evaluation of the experience at the end.

Cara whispered, "Another tree will end up in the bin."

I agreed, using my eyes. We handed out the

sheets. There is no point in discussing the uselessness of this activity with the overlord. He had probably been told to introduce such measures by a think tank or in one of the leadership courses he attended instead of teaching. The kids were not pleased with this either but stayed quiet because they knew any misbehaviour towards an overlord carried higher sanctions than a *this is stupid miss, I won't do it* line they could use on the serfs without much consequence.

"I expect all mobile phones to be turned off immediately. We need you to focus on this learning experience ahead fully."

Some of the kids started turning around, looking at each other and looking at me, Cara and Frank. We were equally taken aback. The letter to parents clearly stated that mobile phones were allowed on the trip and photos could be taken as long as no photos of people who did not want to be included were taken.

I walked over to Cunningham and quietly said, "Sorry to interrupt. The kids had been told they would be allowed to use phones to record their learning experience and take photos of exhibition pieces as well as each other if they wished to do so."

This flustered Cunningham.

"Miss, I do not appreciate you correcting me. This is very unprofessional."

"Mr Josiah organised the trip. With Mr Josiah, I wrote the letter to the parents, having first consulted the Senior Leadership Team, who had granted students permission to use their phones."

I paused, waiting for a reaction. There was none.

"If 200 students cannot use their phones on this trip even though their letter had explicitly told them and their parents they could, we will have a riot on our hands right here in this car park. It will reflect badly on the academy."

I walked back to the line and waited. After a minute, Cunnigham realised that changing his phone policy at this stage may cause an embarrassing scene, which he wanted to avoid since his priority was to uphold the school's image.

"Students, I want to thank Miss for reminding me that your letter stated that you can use your phone on this trip. However, please ensure we respect the members of the public here. Also, remember the worksheet I have created for you. I will collect this back in at the end of the day. Now follow me, please."

Smiles of relief returned to the kids' faces, and the day was saved, at least for now. I was annoyed with Cunningham. Why was he even let out of the factory? He should stick with his data sheets and numbers in some tiny windowless office. He would not notice the sunshine anyway. It showed that he was in the classroom seldom and in his office often. Sadly, the drama did not end here because Cunningham had been allocated to stick with Cara, our 20 kids, and me throughout the trip. We now had 21 kids not to lose.

Mr Josiah had divided up the kids in a ridiculous manner. Rather than ensuring each teacher had kids they actually taught and therefore knew by name and personality, he randomly allocated them into entirely new groups. This made everyone's day harder because we did not know the kids' names. It also appeared that he had made sure that the top kids were in his group, making his day pretty easy because those kids came equipped with pens and curiosity. There was nothing I could do about it now. Cara looked at Cunnigham and then at me; we were both thinking the same. Here goes the free time we had allocated in our heads for a coffee in the cafe whilst the kids spent 30 minutes unsupervised in the shop. The weather did not disappoint, unlike Cunnigham, who kept going on and on about his stupid worksheets. Some kids had already put them in the bin or decorated them with penises.

MONDAY, 2 PM

My favourite parts were the little tour of the canal and the sweet shop. I bought some treats for Bella and myself. The kids seemed to enjoy their day and were relaxed until they arrived at the colliery. They were taken into the mine by an old little man, a volunteer who worked at the museum. He was lovely, but the group turned unruly once in the darkness of the mines. There was screaming and ghost noises.

"Students, you are representing the school. There will be consequences." Cunningham shouted.

Cara and I tried our best to reason with the wild crowd, but they did not care. Not being able to call anyone by their name was equally as unhelpful as Cunnigham's behaviour policy reminders. After ten minutes in the mine, the lovely volunteer terminated the tour. Everyone was returning to ground level, where the sun shone in our faces. Cunnigham wanted the floor to swallow him because his group had been kicked out of the mine. Cara apologised to the volunteer and thanked him for his patience. I took another headcount, ensuring nobody had been forgotten in the darkness of the mines with the ghosts of previous visitors.

Disappointed, the little old man walked off towards the visitor centre. I felt sorry for him. He did not deserve this. Cunningham, ever the overlord, had everyone line up against the wall and marched them off the museum's premises. We had left an hour before we were meant to meet back at the coach. Cunningham had not considered that the coach drivers did not wait on the coaches the entire time. They were nowhere to be seen. Now we had to entertain the kids in the car park. What a great place to be. I wondered whether Mr Josiah had put a prolonged period stuck in the car park on his risk assessment. Probably not. I somehow got the kids to sit by the side of the entrance on the floor. The good weather allowed for it, and what else were we meant to do? I opened the box of coxinhas and handed one over to Cara, who sat next to me on the floor. Together, we enjoyed this delicious snack. Cunnigham stood there, trying to look authoritarian. He reminded kids that there would be consequences and that he may be more lenient in punishing those who completed their worksheets. *Consequences* had become the buzzword of the day. Most kids ignored him and dived into their crisps, chocolates and social media.

Cara shut her eyes and relaxed. I was happy to miss the after-school training session. This Monday's topic was *collaborating with other schools*, which was utterly pointless. Collaborations with other schools were currently the next big thing. Serfs from our factory were forced to go to another local factory to share ideas, teaching strategies and resources. What a fantastic idea made in teaching hell! It meant completing a ten-minute car journey to the collaboration factory in 45 minutes because it took place during school pick-up time. However, serfs complied, and when meetings finally started around 4.30 pm, we had around 30 minutes to find out what we already knew, which was that the other factory taught different exam boards and different topics. There was nothing to share. We promised to send each other some generic resources. This sounded good and gave the appearance of an action plan. The overlords who had planned this circus were oblivious to the waste of time, petrol and energy. Serfs had given up pointing out the obvious that this exercise was rubbish.

MONDAY, 3 PM

Slowly, the rest of the Year 8 kids gathered near their coaches. I started the headcount and registered when Cunnigham interrupted me and grabbed the register from me.

"I have got this, Miss, you may sit down."

"Ok."

I sat next to Frank.

"Arrogant arse," Frank whispered.

I gave him the thumbs up. The kids were hyper, and there was far too much noise for a proper headcount to go on, but Cunningham, clearly annoyed, continued anyway.

"We are good to go." He proposed sitting back down just behind the coach driver and grabbing the microphone.

"Year 8, attention, please. I am sure you found this trip as enjoyable as I did. The few that ruined the end of the day for us will be dealt with tomorrow. To everyone else, well done,"

He looked serious.

"Please use the time on the coach to complete your worksheet. Hand it to me when you get off the coach outside the school. Thank you."

He sat down, the coach drove out of the car park, and I looked forward to a hot shower and a bottle of wine.

Half an hour into the journey, when we were already back on the motorway, I got a phone call from Mr Josiah, who was on the coach ahead of us.

"Miss, Miss," he shouted with panic in his voice.

"The museum called, they have Matthew Price. What happened to your headcount? How could this have happened?"

"What? Cunningham did the headcount. He did not let me do it. Wait, I'll get him."

I quickly walked to the front of the coach, where Cunningham was looking at some data on his laptop.

"Sir, we have a problem."

I handed him the phone. His face turned ashen. The blood drained out of it.

"We'll go back immediately. Our coach will turn around now."

He returned my phone, and I continued talking to Mr Josiah. Cunningham whispered in the driver's ear, whose eyes popped wide open.

"OK, but you must tell them it will probably take 45 minutes."

"Ok, ok, just get us there quickly."

Looking over his shoulder, Cunningham tried

to determine whether the kids had realised what had happened. I walked through the coach and did my headcount. There were 41 kids. We were meant to have 41 kids. This was odd. But it also meant that one of the six coaches had a kid missing. What went wrong?

I called Mr Josiah.

"Sir, we have 41 kids, and we were meant to have 41 kids. One of the other coaches must be missing a kid."

"I know, Miss, I have just realised it is my coach. I counted wrong. I am missing a kid."

He was close to tears.

"Sir, don't worry. We will go and get Matthew Price. We will also work out who on the coach is the imposter, Matthew. Who is missing from your coach?" I asked.

Mr Josiah sounded defeated.

"We are missing Oliver Jones."

"Thank you. He must be on our coach." I whispered and put the phone down.

I went to the front and grabbed the microphone.

"Oliver. Would Oliver Jones please wave his hand?"

In the back of the coach, Oliver sank deeper into his seat. The other kids shouted.

"You got caught."

The coach driver got off the motorway and turned around toward the Museum.

"Miss, are we going back?"

I just lifted my shoulders, pretending not to know, walking towards Oliver.

"Oliver, please come with me," I demanded sternly, escorting him to Cunnigham.

"Sir, we need to tell the kids something. They are starting to work out that something is wrong. They will probably need to inform their parents they will be late."

"I know, Miss, I will do it in a few minutes," Cunningham replied, visibly annoyed.

I turned around and remarked, "Sir, this is Oliver. He got on the coach instead of Matthew Price. Matthew was meant to get on Mr Josiah's coach but did not."

Cunningham listened and thought, what a nightmare this trip had become. He grabbed the microphone.

"Year 8 silence."

Most kids ignored it; they were in Snapchat or Instagram universes.

"Year 8, quiet." This time, he shouted.

The kids put their phones in their laps, looking shocked.

"It turns out that Matthew Price did not get on our coach, but instead, this young man here, Oliver, decided to join us, pretending to be Matthew," Cunningham explained, "Matthew failed to get on the other coach, and now we need to return to the museum and get him. You may want to tell your parents that we will probably arrive an hour later than expected. Thank you, Oliver and Matthew."

Cunningham hung up the microphone. He asked Oliver to sit beside him for the rest of the journey. I did not know whether to laugh or cry, but nearly an hour after we had left the museum, we arrived back at the entrance. In military steps, Cunnigham walked straight to reception to collect a sheepish-looking Matthew. Upon entering the coach, Matthew was booed and laughed at, and none of the grown-ups on board wanted to stop any of it. Just like the kids, we were annoyed too.

Matthew was made to sit in the front. Cunningham was now babysitting Matthew and Oliver and starting criminal proceedings. Both had to write a statement about what had happened and how they had planned their stunt. Cara and Frank were busy handing out bin liners and baby wipes to clean up. I called Mr Josiah and told him we had Matthew.

I was about to call Flora so she could send a message to the parents from our coach letting them know that we would be late when my phone rang. It was Ajinder.

"Eva, Eva, you won't believe this. They are coming. They are coming for us," she said, half shouting ", OFSTED will be in the factory tomorrow. The head got the call just after lunch."

"Please tell me you are joking. I am losing the will to live," I replied," we have kids throwing up right, left and centre, one missing mobile phone. We have been kicked out of the mines because the kids did not shut up when asked to. Now you are telling me the box tickers are coming tomorrow morning?"

Ajinder laughed hysterically ...

EPILOGUE

...and once Eva had overcome this challenge, she started to plan her escape from the factory to live happily ever after.

Printed in Great Britain
by Amazon

51541825R00189